SUCH A DAY
WILL LAST FOREVER
A NOVELLA

Richard P. Mullin

AllrOneofUs Publishing
Baltimore, Md & Huntsville, Al

This is a work of fiction. Similarities to real people, places, or events are entirely coincidental.

SUCH A DAY WILL LAST FOREVER: A NOVELLA

First edition. March 29, 2021.

ISBN: 979-8201664794

Written by Richard Mullin.

To Marian.

I also thank my family of origin, all the people with whom I lived and worked, my classmates and teachers, and later, my colleagues and students. From all of them, I gained whatever insights on life that I have. I offer a special thank-you to Mike Susko, who made me aware of draft2digital, and provided guidance, encouragement, and editorial help throughout this process.

JANUARY 1, 2000, AND the world did not end. We watched TV as the New Year, the New Century, and the New Millennium swept across the world. Everyone breathed easier when the lights did not go out in Moscow. If even the Russkies could get it right, surely we would too. There had been widespread doomsday predictions that computers would shut down all over the world because they would not recognize the number 2000, and many organizations spent tons of money making their computers "Y2K compatible." I'm glad things did not fall apart for many reasons, but most of all because I had been working on a series of stories that trace epochal changes from 1957 to the end of the century. During this time I often thought we were on the eve of Doomsday.

My project began at our forty-year high-school reunion in 1997. My name is Jeff Andrews. You might recognize my name if you are a business and economics geek. I am a writer, but not the kind of writer I set out to be. Oh, my career has gone OK as a writer on business and economics in some decent magazines and journals. But I've had no success in getting my novels published, so I decided to try writing narratives based on the memories of my classmates. Worse, my book on economic history, which I thought would be my major contribution to western civilization, never found its way to publication. My day job consists of teaching composition and professional writing at a pretty good college in the Pittsburgh area.

Often I wished I had gone into journalism, covering business and economic issues for a paper like the Pittsburgh Post-Gazette. This would have been especially rewarding since a friend and classmate of mine was Andy Kuchar, who toiled in the thickest of the jungles that constituted the economics of the time. I imagine I would have had access to him. We remain close, and maybe it's just as well that I did not have occasion to abuse our friendship by prying into his business. Anyway, that scenario can be filed under "what might have been."

We grew up in Frick, PA. In case you're not familiar with our story, here is how we got our name. The town fathers knew that a nearby town named itself after Andrew Carnegie, and he built them a library. They named our town after Henry Frick, but he didn't give them a nickel. The town had previously been called New Mount Vernon. George Washington had owned property there, but a larger town as well as the county already had the name "Washington."

Our 1997 class reunion would mark the beginning of my revived writing career, or so I hoped. The theme of the reunion was based on an old Statler Brothers song, "The Class of '57 Had a Dream." A group of alums got together and wrote verses of the song for our classmates. Most of them were banal, some were funny, some were cruel, and some fit two or three of the categories. I'll mention two of them; one involved me, another Andy.

> "Ruthie runs a nursery,
> Her specialty is weeds,"
> "Jeff is writing essays
> That no one ever reads."
> "Lenny's a policeman
> Who keeps us safe and sound."
> "Andy ran a steel mill
> Right into the ground."
> And the class of '57 had a dream.

Who we Were

Our high school was St. Brendan's. It was a small Catholic school run by the Sisters of Charity, an order that taught at several other schools in the Pittsburgh area and also a nursing school at a hospital in Pittsburgh. The sisters were good teachers and did not put up with any nonsense––our parents backed them all the way. But the sisters dressed in a funny outfit based, I think, on the fashion at the time of their founder, Elizabeth Seton, whom they always called "Mother Seton." They had us pray every day for her canonization, and she was eventually canonized. Back to the costume. It featured a black bonnet that covered their whole head so that no hair showed. Their habit was also black, and we referred to these holy women as "crows"—not to their face, of course.

All of us boys were interested in girls, sports, cars, and mischief, not necessarily in that order. Our futures would be either going to college—many of us dreaming, delusionally, of getting football scholarships to Notre Dame. Other choices involved joining the Army, Navy, Air Force, or Marines. Or we could get on at the mill. (Unfortunately, the railroad wasn't hiring.) The girls were interested in boys, at least we thought they were. We didn't care much about what else they were interested in. As for the future, the girls had options too. A girl could become a secretary, nurse, or teacher. I'm speaking in generalities, of course. I'm describing how I thought we looked from the outside. We were a little more complicated than that, as I, an aspiring writer, was probably more aware of that than most. I will try to show this by describing some of my friends, as they were then, since then, and now—the spring, summer/fall, and winter of our lives.

The Game

An event from our high school days at St. Brendan's that stays with me more than any other is what we always called "The Game." It was a football game between us and Frick High. Ordinarily we didn't play them. They played in the WPIAL, the Western Pennsylvania Inter-scholastic Athletic League. We played in the Catholic "B" league. These were small schools like us—we didn't play North or Central Catholic. (A few years before our time, St. Brendan played against

Johnny Unitas. We didn't know who he was or what he would become. As you probably guessed, he shredded our defense pretty good.)

Frick was a bigger school, and we were considered no match for them. Beating us would not help their quest for a championship. Their coach, a guy named Bruce Shinko, spoke of us disdainfully. He always called us St. Brenda's. His players told us that when he wanted to motivate them, he said something like "The way you bums are playing St. Brenda's could beat you––hike up their skirts and beat you."

When we were seniors, some local business men had negotiated with Coach Shinko to play St. Brenda's as a season opener. Frick usually started the season with an easy game, a public school that they could beat, but some Chamber of Commerce types thought it would be good to increase the interest in the game by playing us. I don't know what they offered Coach Shinko, but I'm sure he did not play us just to be nice. For him, "nice" was a four letter word.

Before the game, Shinko told his squad that he didn't just want to beat St. Brendan. He wanted to prove once and for all that "St. Brenda's Fighting Nuns" were no match for his powerhouse. Their quarterback, Kent Hillman, asked the coach if they could stay in the game even if they were running up the score. Shinko agreed emphatically. He told them that was what he wanted to hear. Maybe they could set some school and individual records.

A writer from a small local paper came up to us at lunch time and told us about this. Most of us were silent, not wanting to give Coach Shinko any bulletin board material, as if he needed it. But Andy Kuchar spoke up: "That's right! Nobody will want to leave this game. You will see two good teams going at each other for forty-eight minutes." Kent told us that when Coach Shinko read the story in the locker room, they all had a pretty good laugh.

When the big night arrived, I was not on the field. I had been on the team but had an emergency appendectomy the week before the season began. I could have sat on the sideline, but I was asked to work in the press box serving as spotter to the PA guy. I was ok with that because it would also enable me to write about the game. After the Frick High Marching Band, a first-class unit, had played some traditional band music, and the Star-Spangled Banner, the two teams came rushing out onto the field. St. Brendan's won the toss and elected to kick off.

All the excitement came down to this electric moment when our kicker Frank Vodnik sent the ball end-over-end to the waiting Frick return man, Dave Craig. He started up the middle, then turned to the right sideline where the Frick team had set up a wall of blockers. Just like that, the score, with the PAT, was 7-0.

Frick's kick-off was a squib along the ground, which caught our guys off guard. Some of the guys up front tried to field it, and after some fumbling tried to lateral it to the backs. Unfortunately, the back guys had come up-field to block. By the time we fielded it, we were in our own end zone and tackled for a safety. 9-0. We kicked off again and Frick set up for the same right sideline for a runback. Our guys bit, and Craig, with some superb blocking, took it up the middle for another touchdown. 16-0. Not much time off the clock, and not a single play from scrimmage.

Our coach, Dante Donatelli, was not much for razzle-dazzle or trick plays. He believed in learning a few things well and executing with precision. The question was whether we were really outmatched as Coach Shinko had predicted. The 16-0 score seemed to confirm this. Sitting in the press box, I told those around me that Coach D would keep the ball on the ground to use up some of the clock and prevent a shellacking.

This time Frick kicked deep, and we took it in the end zone for a touchback. Now we had it first and ten at the twenty-yard line. As I had predicted, the first play was a run up the middles for a four yard gain. The PA squawked *Kuchar the ball carrier. Second and six.* Andy Kuchar was our primary rusher. He was fast, smart, and very powerful. Our center was big Albert Kellerman, and the guards were Lenny Sadauskas and Vinnie Donatelli, who was the coach's son. The left tackle was a big guy named Hughey Davenport—yeah, his nickname was "Couch." He wasn't especially fast, but was strong, and with a lot of coaching became an effective blocker. The right tackle was Mike Carmichael—I thought he had the coolest name, Michael Carmichael. He was a good all-around athlete and often lined up at the tight end position. On these plays Charlie McGinnis, not very big, but tough and aggressive, would fill in at tackle. Back to the game—the next several plays were a litany. "Kuchar the ball carrier, third and two; Kuchar the ball carrier, first and ten; Kuchar the ball carrier, second and seven, Kuchar the ball carrier, third and one. Kuchar the ball carrier, first and ten."

So it went until we were deep in Frick territory and a frenzied Coach Shinko called timeout. His adjustments worked and on the next two running plays Andy was held to two yards total. On third down, quarterback Dennis Keegan, after faking the run, threw to Frank Vodnik. The pass was complete but short of a first down. Coach Donatelli opted for a field goal attempt. Frank "split the uprights," as we cliché laden writers say, and the score was 16-3. We would not be shut out, and more importantly, we took a lot of time off the clock. I suspected also, that the drive might have taken something out of the formidable Frick team.

I want to make an aside about Coach Donatelli. He was a WW II Marine veteran who went to college on the GI Bill. He studied education with a concentration in math and became our high school math teacher. He especially liked geometry, and in his football coaching he emphasized the importance of angles for blocking and fending off blocks. The two kick-off return touchdowns were out of character for a Coach D team. When it happened he was surprised and angry. He could get angry, but never singled out any individual as an object of his wrath. He said the mistakes were a team effort. He took responsibility for what he always called "a lapse in teaching." That particular lapse in kick coverage did not happen again in this game, or any game ever. I should add that he was passionate about conditioning. When we did wind sprints, and wind sprints, and wind sprints, he always reminded us that games last for forty-eight minutes.

After the field-goal, an unsportsmanlike conduct penalty had moved the ball up for the kick-off and Frank put it into the end zone for a touch-back. A run and a pass from Hillman gave Frick a first down. Next after two runs and an incomplete pass, Frick punted. There was no more scoring in the first half and we went into the locker room down 16-3.

In the second half Frick kicked off and we started at our thirty yard line. Coach D had made a major adjustment, bringing fullback Rege Harkins right up next to the quarter back and lining up behind the right guard Lennie. Rege was good at reading blocks, and so Andy was able to gain on almost every play. We moved the ball downfield methodically as we did in the first possession, with Andy carrying on most plays. Coach Shinko called time out to make some adjustments. When play resumed, Rege was on the other side behind Vinnie. On a surprise Kevin handed the ball to Rege, and he broke loose for twenty-one yards. This kept Frick off balance. Shinko called timeout again. We got the ball down inside the twelve yard line and Shinko used his last time out. Now Frick was ready for a run from any direction. Dennis faked a hand-off to Andy, then rolled to his right. He found Mike Carmichael, our right tackle, who had lined up as a tight end, alone in the end zone, and hit him for a touchdown. Now the score is 16-10.

On Frick's next possession, they tried two long passes unsuccessfully. They were still obviously thinking of winning big. On third and ten they connected for twenty yards. After two incompletions and one gain, they punted and downed the ball on our twelve yard line. We worked the ball up-field. When Frick stacks the line, Keegan passes. When they don't, Kuchar runs. We moved the ball methodically up-field, but they stopped us short of field goal range and took over on downs.

I kept notes on every play, but I don't want to get tedious—some of you may think I already have. So I will stick to high-lights. Frick got within field-goal range several times, but went for the touch-down and were stopped. Coach Shinko was still thinking Big Win, not just win. Early in the fourth quarter, the score still 16 -10, Frick was driving the ball downfield and finally looked unstoppable. At our six yard line, they knew we were expecting a run or short pass, and so tried an end-around reverse. There was a fumble and our linebacker, Rege Harkins, fell on it. We were deep in our territory, and there was plenty of time left. Both sides now knew what should have been obvious, Frick could move the ball. After two carries by Andy, we were third down and inches. Both lines were stacked for an epic battle between two very powerful units. Dennis faked the handoff to Andy and then found Mike alone in the flat. He broke a tackle and went the length of the field untouched. After the Pat it was 17-16, us!

Through binoculars I could see that Coach Shinko and the Frick staff looked worried, but they kept their composure, as did the team. After the kick off, they moved the ball up field methodically as they had on the previous possession. But once again, Rege Harkins worked his magic, intercepting a deflected pass at the three yard line. I knew, and I'm sure both benches knew, that Frick was not finished. It was crucial that we get at least one first down and take time off the clock. Frick had no timeouts left, and they were visibly exhausted, dropping to a knee between each play. It was Andy Kuchar's time. "Kuchar the ball carrier" became the PA mantra. Andy moved the ball three, four, five yards on each carry. Dennis squeezed as much time off the clock as he could between plays. Finally, he was able to end the game by taking a knee. St Brendan had pulled off the most unlikely upset.

Looking back, I think that Frick had the better team. Our line was just a little stronger, but Frick had more speed, skill, and depth.

There were two factors that contributed to Frick's loss, besides underestimating our team. One was that the quick 16 - 0 lead led to an early sense of celebration followed by a let-down that they could not overcome. Another was that Shinko wanted a big victory instead of just a victory and went for touchdowns when a single field-goal would have won it. I would not have wanted to be a Frick player when they faced Coach Shinko the next Monday. But they went on to win the rest of their games in the tough WPIAL. We suffered a letdown and lost our next game before winning the rest.

Coach Shinko was a little more respectful after that. He told Coach Donatelli that he wanted a rematch and would like to make this game an annual tradition, but had already scheduled the following year. Before there could ever be a rematch, the Bishop of Pittsburgh broke everyone's heart by abolishing Catholic B League football

THE NARRATIVES

BEFORE I TALKED TO anyone about my narration, I made some notes. I talked to as many of my old classmates as I could. I told them what I was doing and most of them seemed interested in seeing the finished product, although most asked not to be included by name. There were four that I interviewed in depth and I wrote about their experience in the first person, after checking with them, of course. I worked their information into a narrative rather than an interview question-and-answer format. And I usually left out the recurring phrases, "You may remember..." and "as you know Jeff..."

The main character of my account is **Andy Kuchar**. His career in the steel industry is largely a matter of public record, but I wanted to get an understanding of his youth and how he got into the industry, how he rose so high, and what was going on with him outside the public eye. Andy's story is the main narrative. If this were a novel, he would be the protagonist. Other characters who will tell their story and give their version of events are Ruthie, Frank, and Kathleen.

Ruthie's Story: "Such a Day Will Last Forever"

RUTHIE IS THE SISTER of Albert Kellerman, the biggest and toughest guy in our class and the center of our football team. Ruthie was about a year younger, and like Albert, she was big and strong. We used to say, only half-jokingly, that if Albert got hurt, she could have played center. Of course, the nuns and priests would have frowned on that. Actually, she was about 5'8", full-bodied but not fat or bulky. Her arms and legs were smooth, firm, and shapely like most young women athletes, although she never had the opportunity to play team sports. There is an anecdote that I have to tell. I don't think she will get mad at me, at least I hope not. There was a big round stone down by the creek. I don't know how much it weighed, but we often speculated on whether any of us could pick it up. Albert took the challenge and lifted it over his head. Several others tried unsuccessfully. If I remember correctly, Andy succeeded, as did Lennie Sadauskas, and Vinnie Donatelli. One day a bunch of us were there, girls as well as boys. It was a cool, grassy place and a good spot to hang out.

A couple of the guys played a trick on Ruthie. They told her that several of the girls had lifted the big stone to prove that girls were as strong as boys. Ruthie figured if they could do it, so could she. To our astonishment, she lifted the stone over her head. The only one who was not astonished was her brother, Albert. He said that they always worked together on the farm, and when doing chores such as tossing bales onto the truck, he often had a hard time keeping up with her. When Ruthie learned that she had been tricked, she feigned anger—not very well, but actually thought it was pretty funny—and she was rightfully proud of herself.

Before I begin her narration, let me say a little more about her beyond her farm-bred robustness. First of all, she was very pretty;

blond hair, blue eyes, nice healthy-looking complexion. She had a soft personality and an easy smile. I think everyone liked her. If you think I had a boy-hood crush on her, you would not be far wrong. She was more interested in my friend Frank Vodnik. I will let go of my memory of her for a while and let her tell her story.

Ruthie's Story: My childhood was happy—a lot of hard work, but I loved it, being out-doors and watching plants and animals grow. Our family life was very warm although it was strict. My dad was a big guy who could look fierce, and I think everybody was a little in awe of him. Even other farmers and working men, coal miners and steel workers, commented on his strength. But he was actually very gentle. He saw that we kids stayed in line, but he never resorted to corporal punishment. He didn't need to—the look was enough. And he had a roaring voice that could shake your bones. Because we adored him, the fear of losing his approval was usually all the motivation we needed.

My brother Albert was a lot like our dad. He was always nice to me and to the younger kids. Once, when we were teenagers, as we were walking back to the house after a very hard day of work, I was being a royal pain, bitching about some job that I thought he had not done thoroughly enough. He told me to stop, but I kept nagging. Then he approached me with what I took to be a mean look and I thought "uh-oh," but I didn't back down. He just picked me up, tossed me over his shoulder like a bag of feed, and carried me up to the house. I protested by saying "Hey!" In a calm voice he said "According to the Bible, every man must carry his cross." That's Albert!

At school, Albert—it's funny, he was always "Albert," never "Al," both at home and at school. He's married now and his wife and her family and friends call him "Al." Anyway, he had a lot of friends, especially you guys on the football team. He never bullied anyone and didn't like bullies. I was with him once when he saw a kid his age bullying another kid, holding him in a headlock and taunting him. Albert said, "Hey! You like to fight? I do too. Let's you and me fight."

The kid wasn't dumb enough to fight with Albert, but that stopped the bullying. I think he did that all the time. Being the oldest of six, he always took on the protective role of big brother.

Although we had a lot of work to do, my Mom insisted that we be given time for extra-curricular activities at school. My dad was ok with that. So Albert got to play football. There were no sports for girls, but I thought I could be a manager. The managers of the various sports, mostly boys, did things like make sure the field was ready, that the buses were provided, the refreshment stands stocked. There were plenty of managers for football and basketball, and so I offered to manage the cross-country team. It was just a few boys, you Jeff, Frank, and a few others. You didn't really need a manager, and Frank thought the ideas were dumb. But you knew how much I liked Frank, and you convinced him to go along. I was, and still am, grateful. I helped with transportation, took care of the warm-up clothes, and tried to get Frank to notice me.

You and Frank had done well in the previous two years and were expected to do big things as seniors. You had missed the football season because of surgery and I knew that cross-country had become all the more special for you. Frank had come down with a flu bug early in the winter and was having a hard time shaking it. His performance trailed off (pun intended), and he became discouraged and thought about quitting. I wouldn't let him. I took on the role of cheer-leader and motivator. He stuck with it and won second place in the Regional meet. You were first, and I was so proud of both of you.

Just before commencement, there was an awards ceremony. As the football and basketball teams were getting their awards, they not only brought their managers on-stage with them, but actually carried them up on their shoulders. To my disappointment, Frank was out of town that day for a family funeral. I wondered if you would think to ask me to walk up with you. Then I saw you walking toward me with the purposefulness of a fourteen-year-old boy approaching a girl to ask for his first dance. I was glad I would have the chance to walk up with you, but still wished that Frank was with us. When you got near, I felt your arm around me. Were you really going to walk up to the stage with your arm around me? Then I felt myself suddenly lifted up. You had reached with your right arm behind my knees and swept me up. The surprise took my breath away. You told me that I had carried you and Frank psychologically all these months and now you were carrying me. I made a comment about being too heavy. You replied with no apparent sense of irony, "It's my pleasure." Now I yielded to the experience of being carried. Big strong Ruthie being carried like a little girl. I remember clearly, like it was yesterday. I felt a little embarrassed, but it was fun! I'm glad you did it. I felt like I was appreciated and cared for. I even felt some affection toward you, Jeff—can you believe that!

Editor's note: She was an armful all right, but a very pleasant armful. Back to Ruthie's narrative.

That summer after graduation was a very happy time. Most of our classmates were still around; some would go to college in September, and others would join the military. We spent a lot of time together. Some had jobs and I still had my farm chores, but we got together in the evenings and weekends.

One of my best memories was the time out at our place when you and I walked into the barn and saw Joanne and Frank kissing. He had lifted her off of her feet and they looked quite serious. When we saw them, we tried to quietly back out, but they saw us and begged us to stay. Joanne explained that this was as far as they had ever gone, and since Frank was going to join the Benedictines and become a monk, it was her one and only chance to give him a serious kiss. We believed them; I still do. But I took advantage of the situation. I seized Frank in my arms like the predator that I am (ha ha) and gave him a big kiss. I explained that was our only kiss ever—sadly, it was true. You and Joanne said you believed me, and we all started to laugh. Then Joanne said, "We can't leave Jeff out." So she kissed you. She told me that to complete the cycle, I had to kiss you, too. You looked at me with your imploring puppy-dog eyes, so I kissed you, and said, "Now the cycle is complete." Joanne said, "Not quite," and then she kissed me. That's Joanne! The whole sequence struck us funny, and we all started to laugh. I laughed so hard I almost peed my pants.

That summer was happy even during the day when I was working, especially in the early morning. Later, in college, when I was taking an elective art course, I saw a copy of a painting from the Chicago Art Institute called *The Song of the Lark*. It showed a peasant girl going out to work with a sickle in her hand. She stopped, presumably to listen to the lark sing, and her face showed rapture. I think I know how she felt. I loved the songs of common birds like sparrows, robins, and wrens, but especially from woods adjacent to one of our fields, the other-worldly song of the wood thrush.

Sometimes when I thought about all of our happy times a song ran through mind, "Such a Day as This Will Last Forever." It was popular around that time, and Cecelia Prodnik, who was an outstanding singer and belonged to a group that sang old folk songs, mostly German and Slovenian, told me that the song was a translation of an old German song. She taught us to sing it in English and German.

When the summer was over, I was not sorry because I looked forward to going to college. My wonderful parents had saved up some money and, along with scholarships and work-study, I was able to afford it. I would study biology with an emphasis in botany. I didn't know what I would do with my degree—agriculture, horticulture, forestry, landscaping—but growing things was, and still is my passion.

Ruthie Grows

So I went to college and majored in biology with a concentration in botany. I loved working in the greenhouse and the trips to adjacent college-owned woods looking for specimens. The environmental movement was not yet a part of the public consciousness, but concern about pollution was growing among biologists. The air, water and soil were all being poisoned. I remember reading a doomsday article about how, in the not too distant future, the dominant flora and fauna would be dandelions and catfish. A famous cartoon showed a couple arguing about one of them wasting money on luxuries such as food and clothing when they should be preserving their funds for the essentials, bottled water and bottled air.

Rachel Carson's *Silent Spring* came out around the time I started graduate school. She tried to educate the public on the growing poisoning of our world. But one of her key ideas that always stayed with me is that chemists can make lethal concoctions for weeds and insects faster than biologists can detect their long-range effects. One of the effects that she cited was that spraying residential neighborhoods with DDT to save the elm trees could lead to the extinction of song birds. Hence the title of her book. Her voice was heard and now the elm trees are gone, but the birds are still singing.

During this time I kept up an active interest in pollution and it worried me a great deal. I also kept up a correspondence with Frank in the monastery. Since he said that his superiors could open and read his mail, I was careful to avoid sounding like a girlfriend. I always mentioned you as my boyfriend, which was now the truth, and I wrote to Frank about issues like pollution. Over the next several years, Frank began to study philosophy and shared an article he had written called "From a Mechanistic to an Ecological human self-Image." He argued that from the seventeenth to the twentieth century scientists and philosophers saw the world as an intricate machine and we were somehow outside of it and discerning the laws by which it ran. But now we are beginning to realize that we are very much embedded in the natural world and our very existence depends on how we live.

Frank also explained to me how in the early days of the environmental movement, many people, not only Catholics, thought St. Francis of Assisi should be looked on as the patron saint of the environment. You always see pictures and statues of him talking to birds, or singing his hymn to the sun. But a highly respected writer, Lewis Mumford, argued that the patron of the environment should be St. Benedict. The Benedictine motto was *Ora et Labora,* "Pray and Work," and the Benedictines worked to drain the swamps and make the continent of Europe livable. They developed a sustainable agriculture and provided stability for centuries of growth in learning and culture. Frank was proud of the Benedictine legacy and aimed to develop an environmental philosophy while learning as much as he could about biology, especially horticulture.

Frank and I, as well as you Jeff, stayed close and shared a common interest in environmental issues. I know that you, as a writer consulted with him on issues regarding industry and the environment. Andy, as an executive, drew on the insights of you and Frank, who had become Fr. Cyril, O.S. B. We also shared these interests with my brother Albert who kept the family farm, and with my younger brother Joey and his wife, Pauline, who operated a landscaping business.

I think that the ideas that we developed on sustainability were themselves sustainable. Unfortunately, there were a lot of goofy ideas out there that gave environmentalism a bad name and served as a god-send to conservative pundits. Some argued that we should give up, not only cars and electricity, which pollute the air, but give up books, newspapers and magazines because they involve chopping down trees. Others claimed that mosquitos and the rest of the creatures that we consider pests had as much right to live as humans. They even went so far as to claim that germs that cause malaria and other deadly disease had as much right to live as we do. They insisted that the goal of family planning should be ZPG, zero population growth. The most extreme idea was that we should stop having babies altogether because the human race was the enemy of a healthy planet.

The idea that you, Frank, and I came around to was that we don't need perfection, we just need stability and sustainability. And we can acknowledge the value of all living things without pretending that all species are equal.

I put a lot of thought into choosing my career path. I considered getting a Ph.D. in biology and teaching at the college level, or going to work for the government, perhaps the Department of Agriculture or Interior. (The EPA would be created later.) But I knew I wanted to do hands-on work and did not want to get tangled up in bureaucratic red tape. So I decided to start my own nursery business. Albert would run the family farm, but I would have a parcel of land for my business and we helped each other out a lot and had help from family and friends. My dad, Albert, Joey, and I did most of the building of greenhouses and other buildings. Joey and Pauline ran their landscaping business from the same plot of land and we had a nice, symbiotic relationship.

I worked hard to develop a market for native plants. Most biologists understood that native plants are more environmentally sound. They need less water, fertilizer, and pest control than do exotic plants. I became as well informed as I could on sustainable garden practices and arranged to give talks to garden clubs, Master Gardeners, Scout troops, and school groups.

I was beginning to feel like an environmental evangelist. I thought environmental awareness should be a natural for Catholics, but I could not always convince my fellow Catholics of this. I never remember hearing a Sunday homily on our duty to God's creation. Some young Jewish groups saw environmentalism as an extension of their religious commitment. Others, from all faiths, made environmentalism their new religion. This often led to the kind of imbalance that I noted above. I was glad I had the nursery business because it kept my feet on the ground literally and figuratively.

As I kept learning from research as well as my own experimenting, I became aware of several threats to our eco-system. In addition to the dangers from overuse of chemicals and poisons, there was the impending threat of climate change. Of course, the climate constantly changes over time. But the danger lies in changes that occur too rapidly for the flora to adapt. This holds especially true in agriculture, where human habits tend to be more rigid than is healthy. As I kept in touch with biologists from all over the country, I became more and more aware of how invasive plants and harmful insects were marching relentlessly northward. There were many voices sounding the alarm, but there seemed to be just as many voices discounting the evidence. Politicians would recite how, during their college days, scientists warned about global cooling. So global warming is nothing more than the current fad. Some believed that global warming and other environmental concerns were part of a vast plot to give the government more power over our lives. Why listen to scientists when you can find politicians who tell you what you want to hear?

It became impossible to get the word out. So what do you do? In discussing this problem with Frank, he quoted William James: "Hope for the best; work for the best; and take what comes." So that is what I did. I kept up my work, my research, my teaching, and tried to develop a life-style compatible with my deepest scientific and spiritual beliefs. Part of this was adopting a plant-based diet. Some of the men I encountered in my business told me that you can't be strong without eating animal protein. I wanted to challenge them, but never did. I really don't enjoy embarrassing people. I think I could have beaten these guys in most physical contests from foot-races to arm-wrestling matches.

I tried, not always successfully, to avoid being a pain-in-the-butt vegetarian. But I did encourage healthy eating. A common phrase among ecologists and other biologists was that our food system is broken. For commercial reasons, appearance became more important than nutrition. To take one easy-to-understand example, when we were kids, an ear of corn might have a few kernels missing, but the flavor was wonderful. Now the ears of corn in grocery stores are beautiful to look at, but tasteless. Albert tried to keep good corn growing on his farm, but growing corn is expensive in terms of fertilizer, so he shifted mainly to other crops, mostly grains for sale. We kept a large family-shared garden plot for our own food. Albert's wife and I take produce to a farmer's market every Saturday in season. We make some money, but find it a nice social outlet and a chance to trade ideas and gossip with other farmers and gardeners.

Much of the produce that we find in stores is shipped in from California, the Sun Belt, Mexico, and South America. You can find any kind of food at any time of the year. But think of the carbon foot print of all of that shipping and the chemicals used to keep it bug-free, fresh, and having a nice appearance. We Americans were consuming tons of junk food. Maybe worse, we were eating beef laced with DES, a female hormone that made the meat tender, but could cause men to become impotent and women to have breast cancer. I never claimed that eating meat is immoral, although I chose to stop eating it. But the way big food industry treats poultry, hogs, and cattle is a national disgrace. As I mentioned, I try to not be a pain in the butt. I am taking advantage of your story project to vent my feelings. I never preach, but I try to practice what I would preach if I preached.

Looking back, in the spring time of my life, after Frank joined the monastery and I got over my crush on him, I fell in love with you, Jeff. Our life has been good. But I was also in love with the living earth. I loved people, animals, plants, hills, and streams, all of it. I thought I could make a difference. When nature was endangered, I felt like a mother with a child in trouble. Or maybe more like a child with a mother in trouble. I tried to live my life with integrity and dedication to life, but I felt like the world and me both got drowned in the pollution, waste, and chemical assaults. I felt low at times, but never despaired. I had great support in you, in Frank, in my family, and a lot of friends. Frank advised me that once you make a decision, you live with the confidence that you did the right thing and let go of what you can't control. But when I remember the joy of these early days, I think there is a sense in which these days do last forever.

Frank's Story: Work and Pray

FOR AS LONG AS I CAN remember, I had a deep interest in the Church and thought I might become a priest. I didn't wear my religion on my sleeve and I didn't like to think of myself as pious and certainly didn't want other people to think that of me. When discussions of religion came up with non-Catholics, I tried to stay out of it. In one heated argument, when we were in grade school, a friend of ours from the public school called us out: "You guys are Catholic, but you go to movies on Sunday. I'm only Methodist, but at least I don't go to movies on Sunday." Actually, we never thought that we were better than anyone else as Catholics; we just thought that our religion was better than anyone else's.

I remember another grade-school age anecdote from when we were in Boys' Club Day Camp. Most of us were either Catholics or Protestants scattered over four or five denominations. There were also some Jewish kids. We didn't know them very well because they lived in the up-scale part of town. We knew some of their dads as our doctors, dentists, and local retailers. We didn't know they were Jewish because they didn't talk about their religion. Maybe their parents warned them that people would dislike them for their religion. That might have been true at another place and time, but these were more enlightened times. It was Frick, PA in 1950 for Pete's sake. Anyway, it came out that some of them were Jewish. Someone questioned them about pork, "What do you guys have against pork?" The Jewish kids looked uneasy but didn't answer. But Vinnie Donatelli spoke up. He was a muscular Italian kid and when he spoke, we listened. He said, "That makes sense. Just like us Catholics don't eat any kind of meat on Friday, Jews don't eat pork any time." "Good point, Vinnie." We Catholic kids were all nodding in agreement, the Jewish kids looked a little more relaxed, and the poor Protestant kids were scratching their heads trying to figure out why that made sense.

When I said that I was interested in the Church, I didn't mean the institutional power structure. What I liked was the Mass, and the liturgical seasons, especially Advent and Christmas. Also, the celebration of Holy Week and Easter made spring time even more alive. In religion class we read the Gospels. They were an eye-opener. I thought Jesus was pretty cool and would have been more at home with me and my buddies than with a bunch of stodgy monsignors and imperious bishops. In my early teenage years I had made a retreat at a Benedictine monastery and felt attracted to that monastic way of life.

Because I was pretty sure I wanted to join the Benedictines, I didn't date during high school although I went to dances and parties and hung around in mixed company. There were a lot of attractive girls in our class as well as girls we knew from Frick High. Kathleen Whelan, whom we called the "Social Chairlady," told me that Ruthie Kellerman liked me. Ruthie was pretty and sweet. I looked on her as a good friend and felt some twinge of conscience for not responding to her less than subtle overtures. But I had a crush on her best friend, Joanne Donatelli.

Some of the other girls thought Joanne was too pious and a bit flakey. I think they were wrong and most of our classmates liked her. She was fun-loving, friendly and always seemed to be in a good mood. The adjective that always came to my mind was "radiant." She liked physical contact and when she talked to you, she would often emphasize a point by jabbing you in the stomach—a habit she must have picked up from her dad, Coach Donatelli. When talking to father or daughter, which I often did, it paid to have your abdominal muscles in good shape.

Joanne took her Catholicism more to heart than most. All of our classmates at St. Brendan were Catholic but not very aggressive about it. Joanne went to Mass every day, and the Donatellis said a family rosary each evening. She put her faith into action. Her activities included volunteering as a "candy-striper" to visit people in the hospital. When anyone in the neighborhood was sick, or had a baby, or lost a loved one, she would visit and offer to help out with errands and chores, often with her Presbyterian friend, Phyllis Craig. St. Brendan Parish didn't have any social outreach in those days, but Joanne and Phyllis used to volunteer with the Salvation Army at Christmas time.

Here is an anecdote that reveals what most of us guys thought of Joanne. Kent Hillman, the Frick quarterback, was a cool guy, outgoing and charming, and very much a lady's man. He often bragged about his sexual conquests. A lot of guys were sexually active, but it was usually with one girl whom they would eventually marry. But Kent was a predator. Sometimes in listing his conquests he said that St. Brendan girls were often hard to get, but that made them all the more exciting. When he talked like that Andy Kuchar looked like he wanted to punch him in the mouth, but never did. One day Kent brought up Joanne. He would not have mentioned Joanne if her brother Vinnie had been there. Anyway, after describing her in graphic detail, Kent said he would like to "do" her and asked if we could put in a good word for him. In these conversations most of us would be sitting while Kent held court standing. When he made the remark about Joanne, I was seething and started to stand up to confront him. But while I was dithering, Andy Kuchar was on his feet and in Kent's face. "You leave her the hell alone." That would have been enough, but it got better. Albert Kellerman stood up. He was a big old farm boy that nobody would mess with, and Joanne was his sister's best friend. He didn't say a word, and I noticed that he didn't even clench his fists. But the message was clear. That question never came up again. Kent, for his part, apologized without losing any of his aplomb, and segued seamlessly into a discourse on another aspect of his charmed life—his customized Mercury.

I always thought that Joanne would join a convent. Maybe that was part of my attraction to her—her unavailability. During the summer after graduation when she knew I was going to the Benedictines, we often talked. She said that while she loved and admired the nuns, her strongest role models were her parents, and she wanted to follow their example by raising a family. She would go to nursing school and her classes started that summer. Joanne didn't talk much about her faith—her actions spoke for her—but she told me that she thought the nursing profession was a good way for a young woman in 1957 to live out the Gospels.

Back to my own story. According to plans, I went to study with the Benedictines. After two years of college, we aspiring monks were admitted into the order as novices. I look back on my early days as a Benedictine novice as a very happy time. We had wonderful companionship, played a lot of sports, and had thoughtful conversations. I even enjoyed the prayers. We met at regular intervals during the day, "the hours" as they called them, and chanted psalms in Latin. I had liked the liturgy all my life, and no one does liturgy better than the Benedictines. I was enchanted by the rhythm of the day as well as the rhythm of the year.

After the year of novitiate we spent two years studying Thomistic philosophy. This was a time just after the death of Pope Pius XII and the election of Pope John XXIII who convened the Second Vatican Council. Some major changes were just a few years down the road, but among many Catholic intellectuals there was already a lot of foment. Many of my classmates, both Benedictine and the diocesan seminarians who studied with us, were mad as hell. They thought the Church was stuck in the Middle Ages and that it stifled our intellectual and personal growth. I had never thought of it this way. I thought a Catholic is a Catholic, and it never dawned on me that there were opposing conservative and progressive voices.

After two years of general studies and two years of philosophy we finally began studying theology. By now, Vatican II was in full force and there were a lot of exciting things happening in theology, Scripture Study, and liturgical reform. We had some grumpy guys who wanted to keep the Latin and everything else they had grown up with. Someone described these types as "frozen in amber." On the other end of the spectrum there were some real pain-in-the-butt "liturgists." I remember one such guy in particular, a diocesan student, who learned that some of the priests in the Chancery Office were temporarily assigned to parishes. He was concerned that they would get "stuck" out there. How awful! A parish priest being stuck in a parish! This guy planned to spend his career in the Chancery Office handing down mandates to parishes on how to reform their liturgy. I don't know what happened to that guy.

But overall, this was an exhilarating era that felt like a spring time in the Church. I felt so fortunate to be a Catholic at this moment in history. I liked the old Latin, but strongly favored the vernacular. There were a lot of good ideas being generated about participation of lay people in the liturgy and in the administration of the Church. Many of the seminarians were hoping that celibacy would be made optional for priests, and some hoped that women would be admitted to the priesthood. We were reading works by French and German theologians and looked forward to serving a Church that would be stronger and more vital than ever.

After theology and ordination, my Abbot sent me to Yale to study philosophy. Going to Yale involved a lot of hard work, but it was fun. My classmates were among the most stimulating friends I ever had, and the outstanding faculty included John E. Smith, who was reawakening the philosophical community to the wisdom of Josiah Royce. Along with William James and Charles Sanders Peirce, Royce became one of my heroes and exemplars of what I thought philosophy should be. When I read Royce's take on the meaning of "The Beloved Community," I wondered why his thought had not become more pronounced in Catholic theology and whether I could have some influence in making it so. I have written about these ideas and continue to do so. But Jeff let me go on with what you are calling my story.

When I finally got into teaching, the students were interested in the ideas of the American philosophers, but many of my colleagues, both clerical and lay, resented the idea of having an alternative to Thomism. These guys thought that original thinking in philosophy ended in the year 1274, the year that St. Thomas died. All philosophy in Catholic college and universities should be commentaries on St. Thomas. Further, they claimed that American philosophy, with the often misunderstood title of "Pragmatism," was about opportunism and dealt only with mundane questions of material acquisitions and power. When I tried to explain that they were dead wrong, they put their hands over their ears and said "lalalala..." (They didn't do this literally, but they might as well have.)

While the conservatives in the Church and in the larger society despised Pragmatism, there was another philosophy that they absolutely hated. This was Existential Phenomenology, which the philosophy department at Duquesne University was emphasizing. This philosophy was a solid and legitimate approach to reality that grew out of European soil. But the conservatives blamed it on all the dissolution that took place in society and in the Church in late 60s.

I mentioned the dissolution. I still don't know how to explain it. In the early 60s we seemed to be entering a springtime of growth and creativity both for the church and the nation. When John F. Kennedy was inaugurated in 1961, poet Robert Frost called it:

The golden age of poetry and power,
Of which this noonday is the beginning hour.

But then our country suffered a series of shattering events, the first of which was the assassination of President Kennedy in 1963, followed by assassinations of Malcolm X in 1964, and both Martin Luther King and Robert Kennedy in 1968. The escalation of the war in Vietnam along with deadly riots in many American cities, chaos on college campuses, and the bloody riot at the Democratic convention in

Chicago, all contributed to things falling apart. I didn't understand and still do not fully understand what were the causes and what were the symptoms.

I thought a lot about how things fall apart and tried to write about it. I won't go into detail here, but generally we experienced a major shift in consciousness. Other such shifts in modern history include the Renaissance, The Reformation, The Enlightenment, The American and French Revolutions, and the Progressive movement in Europe and the U.S., as well as the Communist Revolutions in Russia and later in China. In all these cases the consciousness of some, especially the better educated and the young moves away from the conventional thinking. Those who are prospering or at least feel content with the existing order resist, and violence usually results.

In the crises of the 60s, men who had gone to war in Europe or the Pacific could not understand why their own sons and other young men refused to fight in Viet Nam. Prosperous white people in the south, who believed that black people were doing just fine, could not understand why "outside agitators" were stirring up trouble—unless they were Communists. College deans and presidents who thought they provided curricula and living quarters that any reasonable person would be thankful for were taken aback by the demands of their students. As I watched this unfold on my own campus, I tried to understand and mediate.

I am by nature conservative—I like tradition and do not like disruptive behavior. But I knew that the parties making demands, whether students, racial minorities, draftees, or women, all had legitimate beefs. I thought those in power should listen, try to understand, and meet any legitimate grievances. On campus I tried to say this to the power holders in the administration. Their reaction? Hands over the ears "lalalala…"

In the years that followed, life did not measure up to our early hopes. As one of my colleagues phrased it, "I see my golden dreams turn brown before my eyes." Reform of liturgy gave way to "experimental liturgy." The Church became a circus—heavy metal bands at Mass, chasubles with Snoopy the dog, priests scoffing at devotions, such as the rosary, that meant a lot to older parishioners. I kept hoping that when we got through this, we would have something better than we ever had. In a way we did, but much of the vitality had gone out of the Church. People started falling away, vocations dried up, and priests began leaving in droves. As one colleague put it "Those wedding bells are breaking up that old gang of mine."

I enjoyed the life that I had chosen. My teaching went well, and I related well to students who were concerned with the changes in the Church, the problem of racism, and the war in Vietnam. In 1968 political activism abounded. Many students were divided between Robert Kennedy and Eugene McCarthy. Of course there were Nixon supporters, but they tended to keep a lower profile. By 1972, the interest in politics had virtually disappeared. I didn't understand why, and I'm still at a loss. I think it was mainly a matter of disillusionment. The civil rights movement culminated in the burning of many American cities, the violence by the police at the Democratic convention in Chicago precipitated a loss of trust in government, and the war in Vietnam was winding down and Richard Nixon would get the credit for ending it. The students with their psychedelic music and some chemical aids were turning in on themselves.

In the years that followed, more and more of my friends and colleagues were leaving the priesthood. Some of them were leaving the Church. I had thought, when I made my solemn vows, that my life was set. But now I was feeling a great uneasiness, more of an emptiness. The monastery and the Church itself were not what I had remembered; it was like the life had gone out of it. I was stirred by something I had read in Carl Jung. He was not Catholic, but he thought that the definition of the Doctrine of the Assumption, in the 1950s was an important moment in the religious consciousness of the west. The doctrine said that Mary was assumed into heaven. Jung argued that since Mary is a symbol of the Church, the Church itself was assumed into heaven, and what was left was a shell. We were at the dawn of a new age of religious consciousness. I didn't know if Jung was right, and I still don't, but it sure felt that way to me.

I had always been faithful to my vow of celibacy, but my mind often wandered back to Joanne Donatelli. She is a nurse and married to a doctor whom she had met while working in a poor area of Mississippi. The two of them were dedicated to their faith and to the poor. They had a family and would take turns going off to Mexico or Central America or to Africa to tend the health needs of those who would otherwise go without it. Joanne was better off with him than with me because I don't know if I could have done that. Since my life was aimed toward philosophy and theology from a young age, I don't know what I would have studied if I had not gone to the monastery. Probably one of the sciences and not medicine.

I went through a tumultuous period of indecision. I have always been the kind of person who keeps commitments, and I had committed to being a monk for my whole life. But now the landscape of my life was changing. I was beginning to feel like an empty shell going through the same motions without the Spirit motivating me. I began to wonder if I had fulfilled my calling and now there was another call. When I thought about leaving the monastery and the Benedictine Order, the words of Robert Frost kept running through my mind: "Unless I'm wrong, I but obey/ the urge of song, I'm bound—away." Contrary to the advice of my spiritual director, I felt like the spirit was calling me to move on and that staying would have been in a way sinful.

I went through the proper channels of applying for a dispensation of my vows. As the saying went, I did it "by the book." I resolved in my mind that I would wait, but I would not wait forever. Fortunately, the dispensation came in a reasonable length of time. As for my work-life, I was at a loss. I had tenure, but both the Dean of the college and my religious superiors made it clear that it would be better for both me and them if I left. I agreed. I was leaving the monastery and the priesthood to start a new life, not to cling half-heartedly to the old. The Abbot loaned me some money to get on my feet—a loan I accepted gratefully and have since paid back. I then applied for and was accepted into a physician's assistant program and that has been my livelihood since the time I left the monastery.

I will never forget how I felt when I made my decision. I experienced a joy that I had not had before. It was spring, and I noticed the beauty of all the blossoms and, for the first time in my life, realized how beautiful the song of the robin sounds. I now knew that beauty in nature consists of something much more than light refracting from things, as the materialists believe. I saw beauty in trees, flowers, buildings, paintings, and, most of all, in people. I heard beauty in bird songs, human voices, and music.

I undertook my medical studies with the same energy and excitement as I had done with my study of philosophy decades ago. Most of the students were considerably younger and looked at me mostly with amusement. One young lady thought it was "cute" that I had come back to study something at my age. When the students learned that I had been a philosophy professor, many of them said that they loved their undergraduate philosophy course and some of them expressed interest in "the big questions." We philosophers think about and debate the relation of the individual and community. When I interpreted my own thought to my new profession of health care, I pointed out that you cannot be good in any aspect of health care without contributing to the good of the community, and you cannot contribute your particular good to the community without becoming very good in your individual skill and knowledge. The students usually did not greet this insight with "Wow! I never thought of that." It was mostly "Well duh, it's what we all know."

My social life was problematic. I was in my forties and had never even asked a girl out. I was too old for my classmates. When I went home to visit my old friends, you, Andy, Dennis, Albert, you were supportive, but seemed uneasy not knowing exactly how to talk to an ex-priest. I threw myself into my work, and although I found a lot of the women doctors and nurses attractive, I acted cautiously. I was old enough to understand how infatuation can be mistaken for love. But then this happened.

I received a phone call from Joanne who was very distraught. Her husband, working with Doctors without Borders, had contracted an infectious disease and died. I felt terrible for her and her three kids, and I wanted to do whatever I could. She came back to Frick where she had strong family support. I wanted to be supportive without being intrusive, but she invited me to join in their family gatherings. Her dad, Coach Dante, was still healthy but did not move around as easily as before. Her mom was still beautiful. Her brother Vinnie was married, had a family, and was a successful engineer. The younger brother and sister were also married and doing well. The whole family treated me as one of them. I figured that my relation with Joanne could never be more than a friendship, but my new calling apparently meant being there for her and an uncle figure for her kids—not that they didn't have natural uncles who were also very generous with their care.

Joanne and I began spending more time together and our friendship deepened. You know the rest. I had been in love with her since we were teenagers, but I thought that when we went our separate ways—she to a very good marriage, me to the monastery—my feelings toward her were just a happy memory. I never thought it would come full-circle like it did, and I am honestly sorry that it was under tragic circumstances. But it did come full-circle. After more than a year of making sure it was not just a rebound, we got engaged and are now happily married. I had some happy times in my life—life has been good to me. But I am happier now than ever.

YOU ASKED ME TO SHARE my memories of our days in at St. Brendan on the grounds that I knew everybody. Some people called me the "Social Chairlady." I wasn't crazy about that moniker, but I didn't let it bother me. It's true that I knew everybody and knew a lot about most of my classmates. It's also true that I did not like to see anybody left out and always did my best to make sure that everybody was included in social gatherings.

Looking back, I understand how my attitude developed. I was the middle child of three girls. My older sister, Rosemary, was beautiful, smart, and talented. My younger sister, Margie, was very pretty, charming, and had a pleasantly gushing personality. In addition, she was quite good at music and art. I did not consider myself to be ugly, dumb, or klutzy, but let's just say that in the Whelan family I was the third prettiest, third smartest, and third most talented. Bronze all the way! When we had friends or relatives visiting, which seemed to be all the time, I felt invisible.

My parents were fair, nurturing, and affirming, but I was especially blessed by the fact that my grandfather took me under his wing. Everyone called him "Big Jim." He was about 6'2" with broad shoulders and stove-pipe forearms. He was active in local politics and embodied the proto-typical Irish politician. He knew everybody and made them feel that he was truly interested in them, which, by the way, he was. Back in his day he was a force in union organizing, in various business ventures, and in the building of St Brendan Church and school. He had two terms as mayor of Frick and served a term as a county commissioner.

I often wondered why Big Jim didn't go further, governor or senator. My Dad explained that Big Jim was happy and effective in Frick. His talents were greater than his ambition. There are more than enough people in politics and government whose ambitions outstrip their talents. Anyway, Big Jim doted on all his grandchildren but I think he singled me out. Rosemary and Margie agreed with my assessment, but didn't show any resentment—they were both busy shining in their own orbits. Big Jim often took me places with him and I watched him interact with people and deliberately absorbed his charm.

As a parenthetical remark, there was one downside to going places with Big Jim. Every time he took me somewhere, on the ride back he would sing "I'll Take You Home Again Kathleen." Every time! Every *(expletive)* time! But that was a modest price to pay for all that he did for me and all that I learned from him.

I also learned early in life that since I didn't draw people to me, I had to reach out to them. I got in the habit of approaching everybody and finding out what made them tick. If I saw someone alone, I would invite them into our group. I did this for girls if it was a group of girls, and for boys and girls if it was a mixed group. I had some close friends. Cecelia Prodnik had an outstanding singing voice and Ruthie Kellerman, Joanne Donatelli, and I had decent voices. We used to sing together all the time in private and any chance we could get in public.

The four of us were very close but Cecelia was my best friend. Besides being blessed with music talent and a solid work ethic for developing it, she was drop-dead gorgeous. A lot of girls were pretty, but she was in a class by herself. Some of the girls were jealous and accused Cecelia of being conceited and stuck up. She was neither. A comment that they often made was "She is beautiful, and she knows it." Well, yeah! How could she not know it if she had access to a mirror? But she never praised herself or denigrated other girls.

Kathleen on Cecelia and Dennis

Aside from envy, one reason a few girls might have resented Cecelia is that she seemed to be moody. I think that she worked so hard on her singing and on various rehearsals and performances, that she was often exhausted. Part of our friendship rested on the fact that she knew that I understood her and could always be there for her. She was very generous with her time and talent singing in Church, at weddings and funerals, and in local musicals. She teamed up with her boyfriend Dennis Keegan who had movie-star good looks and was also a good singer and performer. Over the years they must have taken on the role of the central couple in almost every musical you ever heard of, not just in Frick, but throughout the Pittsburgh area.

Their reputation grew beyond western Pennsylvania and the Tri-state region. It looked like they might make it big as invitations for auditions came from several places, especially New York. An invitation to New York became a game-changer. This one was just for Cecelia, but Dennis was very supportive and encouraging. It was going well until Cecelia told Dennis that the producer had come on to her in a very aggressive way and that she no longer thought she could work for him. Dennis was not especially hot-headed, but this was too much. He beat the crap out of the producer. Now he was in trouble. The producer worked out a deal that he would not press charges if Dennis agreed to keep quiet about the whole affair. Cecelia told the story to me in confidence, and I kept the confidence as long as the producer was alive. I still won't use his name.

After this, the invitations and auditions suddenly stopped; their hope for stardom was over. Dennis regrets his agreement although it seemed at the time to be the only thing he could do. But he feels bad that his silence enabled the producer to continue his assault on other young women looking toward theatrical careers. Dennis now thinks that beating up the producer, though satisfying, was the dumbest thing he ever did. He made amends by going to law school and specializing in representing women who claimed sexual harassment or discrimination. Cecelia became a teacher of music and voice and the two of them directed and acted in a lot of amateur theater. They have a beautiful family—that's a surprise—and they are both very happy now.

Back to Kathleen

Continuing my story, I didn't date much in high school; actually, I didn't date at all. Anytime there was a dance or a party, Andy Kuchar hung out with me. Everyone assumed we were boyfriend and girlfriend, but he never asked me out on a date and never expressed anything romantically beyond dancing. I was all right with that. I enjoyed Andy's company, and he apparently enjoyed mine. I had a lot of friends, and as I stated above, some very close friends. (Don't tell anybody, but I was in love with Andy.)

The summer after graduation, Andy finally took me out to dinner and to a show at the Civic Light Opera in Pittsburgh. He told me that he thought we could have a future together. He would fulfill his military duty by volunteering for the draft for a two-year hitch. After that he would go to college to study engineering. He asked me if I thought I could wait for him. Yes! At the end of the evening he gave me a respectful but hearty kiss. I was glowing for some time after that. I was not totally surprised. As I said before, I was always pretty good at reading people. I just did not want to slip into wishful thinking. Andy and I kept in close touch. After the army, he went to Carnegie Tech to study industrial engineering, I went Duquesne to study psychology and then got a Master's degree. After college, he got a job, I continued working on my doctorate and we got married.

After completing my doctorate, I went to work as a therapist for a clinic. My supervisor, a nun in her fifties, quickly became my mentor. She affirmed the work that I was doing early in my practice, but told me that true clinical wisdom consists in whatever you know after you have forgotten what you learned in graduate school. Early in my career, I liked the various theories that I had leaned and tried to match the most appropriate theory to each client. But in time I learned that the theory doesn't matter as much as the rapport that you establish between yourself and the client. Theories are helpful in providing structure, but you shouldn't become dependent on them. I thought of the analogy of the handrail on a set of steep stairs. The handrail can provide some stability, but you have to do the climbing.

For the therapy to be effective, the client must see the therapist as someone who cares about them unconditionally. Next they begin to see themselves as valuable and worth saving. Further, they have to develop the faith in themselves, the belief that they have the resources to solve their problems and improve their life. Only then can you help them form a strategy for short range and long-range improvement. I loved counselling and equally love the opportunity to teach undergraduate courses.

Later, when I was in my mid-thirties, a third branch of my career opened when some young women approached me about becoming their life coach. They were friends of each other, so I decided that a group might be the best way to handle their needs. These were women who did not have what we call "clinical problems," but who thought they needed a boost in fulfilling their potential. This was at a time when women were entering fields where there had not been much of a female presence before. One of them said that my role would be that of a big sister, which was ironic since I had always thought of myself as the quintessential middle kid.

According to the Adlerian theorists, the birth order in your family of origin is crucial. Being the middle kid helped me to understand vertical relationships both higher and lower. In relationship to a boss, it is important to be respectful and cooperative, but never subservient or worshipful. The danger looms especially with a young woman and a male boss. Aside from the danger of sexual exploitation, the boss might resent a woman crashing the boy's club, or think that she is cute for wanting to be like the boys. Negative behavior can range from patronizing to abusive. Of course not all male bosses fit the above description. Many are very fair and supportive to all young employees, male or female. I am married to such a guy.

Some thought that more women in authority would solve the problem for young women in previously all-male professions. Sometimes this is true. I knew of women, both from personal acquaintance and from reading, who become mentors So my original advice to all young women and men as well, whether the boss is a man or a woman, "Be respectful and cooperative, but never subservient or worshipful."

As for dealing with subordinates, this is an area that can be a mine field. On one level, treat them with the respect that you wanted as a beginner, or the way you would want a boss to treat your younger sister or your daughter. But don't assume that they are just like you were at their age; don't impose you values or your personality on them. Talk to them so you get to know their wants and needs, and as long as they are doing the job that they are hired to do, abiding by generally accepted ethics and the ethical code of the company, let them be. Give them some room to grow, but let them know that you are supportive. Otherwise get out of their way.

For Andy and me, our life went well. I had a satisfying career filling an important need. Andy was phenomenally successful as a steel executive. Our family grew and all four kids did well in their career and marriages. Then things fell apart.

Our family did not fall apart, but the steel industry did. Andy had given everything he had to keep the mills running and to keep them in Western Pennsylvania. When he failed, he was accused by some ignorant people of betraying the workers. Andy had always prided himself in being able to control things in his sphere of influence. But now he was watching his world disintegrate and there was nothing he could do about it. His whole notion of himself was shaken. He was never abusive toward me aside from being grouchy and short-tempered. But we both maintained our mutual love and loyalty. It hurt me to see him suffer so much and in spite of my reputation as a counsellor, I couldn't do anything about it.

I GREW UP IN A BLUE-collar family with three brothers and a sister. My parents prided themselves with how hard they worked and the opportunities they provided for us kids. My dad was a hands-on owner of a small construction business which, as he explained, was big enough to keep us financially well off, but not so big that it would take his time and attention away from the family. My mother kept the books and tended the business side of the operation. All of us boys learned the basic construction skills such as carpentry, plumbing, and electrical wiring.

My older brother Louis, made the business his full-time employment and would eventually inherit it. Besides work, his passion was volunteer fire-fighting. The whole family was involved with the fire department and Louis would eventually become chief. My younger brother, Joe, liked to think big, and with my parents' blessing, he started his own business. Unlike our dad, he did not resist the temptation to make it grow. It would soon eclipse the family business. Joe was always on good terms with my dad and Louis, and sometimes sub-contracted jobs to them. My youngest brother, Pete, went to the seminary to study for the dioceses of Pittsburgh. Our sister, Pauline, helped my mother with the office work and also learned some of the construction skills at which she was pretty darn good. But her special interest was landscaping. She and her husband, Joey Kellerman, would later start their own landscaping business.

As the second oldest boy, I had to find my own niche. Louis was big, well-behaved, but not especially interested in school. He loved manual work, firefighting, and had a fascination with the sea. After high school he enlisted in the Navy and fulfilled that side of his nature. Now he would throw himself into construction work in land-locked Frick. I found my niche by devoting myself to school work. I also played sports and kept myself physically fit. We Kuchars had some natural brawn, but I wanted more and worked hard at developing strength and stamina.

I bought a set of bar bells and dumb bells. My dad was skeptical and asked me if I aspired to be a circus strongman. But he didn't interfere with my plans. I just wanted to increase my athletic ability. I didn't have any very heavy weights, but I built up my stamina by doing a lot of reps.

My favorite sport was football. Coach Donatelli said I was made for the game. I often felt like the game was made for me. I played running-back and loved the feeling of breaking through the line of scrimmage and penetrating the defensive backfield. I wonder what Freud would say about that. I was a guard on the basketball team. I didn't start but was the seventh man and got a lot of playing time. In baseball, I was the catcher. I had a good throw to second and was pretty effective at blocking home plate.

I took my academic work very seriously. There were five of us who stood on top academically. I never had the deep curiosity and love of learning like you and Frank had. Nor was I inspired by a desire to know the beauty of God's creation like Ruthie and Joanne were. For me it was the challenge. Give me an assignment to do, or a subject to learn, and I stayed with it until I got it. That worked for me and I enjoyed it.

During high school, I didn't date girls. My desires were very strong, but like everything else in my life, I wanted to keep them under control. That's probably why I played sports and studied with such passion. Kent Hillman and I were friendly toward each other and he was very cordial and fun to be with. He openly bragged about his sexual activity. A part of me resented him, but in a way I felt envious and even found myself admiring him. But I did not believe that his life-style was ok. I guess that's the Catholic in me.

I liked a lot of the girls whom I knew, but I thought it was better for them and for me if we did not go out alone. Ruthie was a sweetheart with her down-to-earth warmth and charm. I knew that you always liked her, and I didn't blame you. Who couldn't love Joanne with her passion, vitality, and love of life? She seemed to love God, people, and all creation, a trait I have always found attractive. As for Cecelia, what Frank described as "her ethereal and yet sensual beauty" was almost overwhelming. However, she was always very nice, and I liked her. But the one I liked most of all was Kathleen. We didn't date, we were just friends, but I admired her outgoingness and the way she looked out for everybody. I hung around with her at parties, picnics, and other social occasions. I visited her house as often as I could, but always with friends, usually you or Frank or several of us. She had two sisters who, like Kathleen, were very pretty, vivacious, and affectionate. Her Mom and Dad made all of us feel like they were our parents too. Often Kathleen's grandfather, Big Jim, would stop by. We all knew stories about him, but he did not talk about himself. He asked us about our interests and made us feel like we were the most important people he knew.

My friendship and affection toward Kathleen kept growing until sometime during our senior year it occurred to me that I was in love. I hoped it was mutual, but I couldn't ask her. The friendship was certainly mutual, but I was now hoping for something more. After we graduated, I finally took her out.

That evening I spilled my gut and told her that I would go into the Army and then college, but that she was part of my long-term plans. She agreed emphatically and, to my delight, she did not try to hide her enthusiasm at this prospect. During our college years I can say, without going into detail, that we became definitely boyfriend and girlfriend. Marrying her was the best thing I ever did.

I studied engineering and decided I wanted to make my career in steel. I grew up in Western Pennsylvania and was always proud of our heritage. As a kid I loved seeing the flames from the Bessemers and thought there could be no better industry to work for. In college I managed to get summer internships in the mill, and I read everything

I could get my hands on to make myself at least a minor expert on steel-making.

After I graduated from Carnegie Tech with a degree in mechanical engineering, I applied for and got a job at US Steel. I threw myself into my work as I have always done, making sure that I was doing more than I was paid to do. At the same time I continued to learn about the industry. Among other things I read about Andrew Carnegie and the historical foundation of the company and the industry. Carnegie portrayed himself as a secular saint, and while his own self-image may have been overblown, there is much to admire about him, specifically the fact that he always invested his profits back into the industry keeping it on the cutting edge of technology.

Another important thing I learned from Carnegie early on, is the need to understand people. He said he did not understand steam-operated equipment very well, but he understood the most complicated piece of machinery of all—the human mind. My expertise was the opposite. I understood machinery very well, but my knowledge of how people think and act was average at best. Fortunately, I had married a first-rate expert on the human mind. Kathleen understood people from her childhood and adolescence and that understanding was now supplemented by a PhD in psychology. I took some of my personnel question to her and she coached me along very nicely. I learned quickly, so that I became pretty good at knowing people on my own.

My work did not go unnoticed, and I rose up through a series of promotions to be the assistant director of operations. Before the age of forty, I received an offer from Western Pennsylvania Steel (WPS) to an executive position with the promise of being groomed to be a CEO. I talked this over with my bosses. They were supportive of my move. I was very grateful to them although some cynics among my friends said they were merely getting rid of a potential rival to their own positions. Either way it worked out well for me—or so it seemed.

In the early years of my career, the steel industry was flourishing. I was happy and proud to be a part of it. When I look back on those days, I think of the lyrics of a song that was popular at the time; "Those were the days my friend, I thought they'd never end." Of course, it was not all sweetness and light. We faced a lot of problems, but I found the problems challenging in a way that energized me and often gave me a sense of satisfaction and pride for what I considered a job well done.

Several social issues came to light in the sixties. Chief among them were urban decay, poverty, race and gender discrimination, and environmental pollution. The term "social responsibility of business" came into our vocabulary. Many business leaders held that the only responsibility of business is to maximize profit as long as they are doing so legally and without obvious unethical acts involving force or fraud. Those who held this position were backed by conservative pundits including the highly respected Catholic philosopher, Michael Novak. The premise of these thinkers was that everyone in management, from the CEO on down, was working for the owners—the shareholders. As such, their only moral duty consisted in making sure the "owners" received the best possible return on their investment. If some big-hearted people in management wished to work on "social problems," they could do so on their own time with their own resources.

I had other concerns. For one thing, a lot of young people were becoming disillusioned with the whole business system. Yes, call them "spoiled kids who think that Omaha Beach is a movie about spring break," but these young men and women were coming on, and many of them were asking serious questions. They were often very smart and seriusly dedicated to what they believed in. I thought it would be better for the future of the business economy if we did not lose a whole generation of the brightest young people. Worse, what if they did not just drop out, but used their knowledge and political power to work against us? I learned from Frank, who was teaching ethics, that while a lot of philosophers who wrote about business ethics, were just writing for their fellow philosophers, some business leaders were seriously tackling the problem of social responsibility. I brought myself up to speed on this literature.

I had hired David Craig as my CFO. He was a boyhood friend from my old neighborhood in Frick, and I trusted him like I would one of my brothers. David had studied accounting and built up an impressive resume. As a devout Presbyterian, he strongly believed that the market economy was the best means of creating a better world. Further, he saw the accounting profession as the special guardian of that system. I told David that although I was not the most devout person he ever knew, I deeply believed that following Catholic social teaching was a good way to do business. I picked up this attitude from several sources: my parents, teachers, and professors, my younger brother Fr. Pete, Frank, and even from you Jeff. Yes, we had to make a profit, but that was not our only reason for being in business. David got irritated with me. Since he and I had been lifelong friends, we could be very blunt with each other.

David said he admired Catholic social teaching as a guide for an individual in living justly. In fact, he had even drawn frowns from the Elders in his Presbyterian Church for using Papal Encyclicals in his Sunday-School classes. But he argued that you could not use them to run a business. First of all, he argued, Capitalism is a Protestant way of doing business, with the emphasis on individual responsibility. "For us, business is a calling. Second, the measure of success and failure had to be quantitative, and that meant we had to meticulously follow the profit-and-loss criteria. Earning a profit was not only doing justice to our investors, but also an indicator of prudent stewardship of our resources. It meant that we were producing more than we were consuming. If we try to make decisions based on subjective criterion and squishy thinking, we could run off the rails and not even know it.

I came back at David saying that I understood that there is comfort in numbers because numbers are certain. But they are certain because they are abstract, and reality is concrete and never certain. I argued that you could not put a price or cost-benefit analysis on things such as justice, the health and safety of workers and consumers, and environmental stewardship.

David replied that if we keep our eyes on our duty to work profitably, all of these problems will be met. For one thing, to hire the best and most productive men and women, we would have to avoid discrimination. For the same reason, we would have to keep our work environment free of danger as well as free of any kind of harassment. To sell our products profitably we would have to concentrate on quality as well as safety. As for the environment, we all live here. We cannot work profitably without clean air and safe drinking water as well as suitable recreational opportunities.

I understood David's arguments, and in spite of my personal respect for him, I thought that they were rather weak—I still think so. I explained to David that, although we disagreed, I needed him to keep me focused on reality. I promised that I would always listen and try to understand his advice, and that I would only disagree if I had good reasons, and I would share my thinking with him. David, always a realist, was ok with that.

The first problem that we confronted was racial discrimination. A delegation from the NAACP demanded and received an invitation to meet with me and Craig to discuss their grievances. Jobs in basic steel paid well and although we had some black workers, they were fewer than the proportion of black people in the area. I looked into the history of hiring, and although I did not find proof of discrimination, most of the jobs were based on family and friendship, and blacks were for the most part shut out. Given the level of prejudice in the forties and fifties, I did not doubt that the discrimination was, at least in part, deliberate. I was relieved to find that those few blacks who were fortunate enough to have been hired, received the same union pay-rates and seniority rights as the white workers.

We met with the NAACP group, and after a little huffing, puffing, and posturing on both sides, we agreed to a plan. We would actively recruit in black neighborhoods and schools and hire one black for each new white hire until our workforce was racially proportionate to the area. Craig backed me all the way. When I made the announcement, I had a member of the United Steelworkers International as well as a local union official by my side. I worried about the reaction of some of the employees who had counted on getting jobs for sons, nephews, and friends. There was some grumbling, cussing, and even some unflattering cartoons of me posted around. I made it clear that while I did not appreciate the cartoons and despised the posting of them, I would not waste time trying to get revenge. But I would not tolerate any cartoon or any other behavior that is racist. David and I kept in close touch with the workers, listening to their grievances, and nothing bad happened.

The next wave of protests and problems had to do with gender. Up to this time a steel-worker was a man, and a secretary was a woman. We set up some reasonable physical tests and affirmed that any man or woman who passed them was eligible for hiring. There were some women who qualified although not a lot. Again, we made it clear that we would not tolerate any misconduct toward the women, and of course, their pay scale and seniority were part of the union contract. You and Frank kept me posted on the literature in this field and we organized workshops to clarify what constitutes sexual harassment and why it would not be tolerated. We must have done something right because there were no lawsuits over harassment or discrimination.

I had one bad experience involving my attempt to mentor a woman in management. A lot of women called "feminists," were pointing out that business board rooms looked like boy's clubs. They were demanding that women take an equal share in corporate leadership.

I was up enough on the times to realize that these women were not going away and that they had a legitimate point. So, just as I had taken action to increase the number of black workers and managers, I also deliberately strove to increase the number of women in management.

There were professional recruiters, commonly called "head-hunters," who would try to match talent with opportunity. One such recruit especially impressed me. I'll call her "Jane." She was a young woman who had received an engineering degree from Purdue and then gone to Wharton for an MBA. Her resume included a stellar academic career, considerable campus leadership roles, a highly successful apprenticeship and strong personal recommendations. She wanted to work in the steel industry and was determined not to get shunted into a traditionally women's industry such a children's clothing. For my part, I felt fortunate to have her on board and was resolved to help her develop as one of the next generation of steel executives.

Because of her background in engineering, I put her in charge of the engineering department. We had some top-notch engineers, all men, whom I thought she could learn from. My long-range plan was to give her a variety of assignments so that she could grasp the whole operation. I have to admit that I was very proud of what I was doing. There is an old saying, "Pride goeth before..." I don't remember the rest of the saying, it was "before glory," or "before success," or some such thing.

As part of my mentoring, I gave Jane a copy of a popular book on management. This bit of largesse came back to bite me. The real leadership in our engineering department came from a classmate of mine, Mike Carmichael. It might sound like I staffed my office with old cronies, but there were just two, Dave Craig and Mike. They both had impeccable academic and professional credentials and track records. And I knew I could trust them and work well with them. Mike had discovered an especially bright engineer name Milt Weitzman who could solve problems that baffled even good engineers. Milt had an edgy personality and an annoying sense of humor, but Mike got along with him, and together they were very efficient, effective, and productive. I always worried about losing Milt as well as Mike to a higher bidder although I would have tried to match any competitor. As it was, I paid them well because they were worth it.

Then this happened. At a routine progress-report meeting, Jane informed me that she had fired Milt. I was aghast. When I asked why in the hell, she stiffened and told me that the book I had given her recommended that a woman in an executive position, in order to be taken seriously by an all-male staff, had to fire someone early in her tenure. I was seething but determined to keep cool on the outside. She sensed my discomfort and she was very skilled at manipulation. She asked if I was serious when I had assured her about being in charge, or was she a token affirmative-action female? Further, had I not read the book I gave her? (I had read it but never thought that anyone would fire a person without cause.) She went on to say that she had a hard time getting along with Milt (most people did) and that his presence was upsetting the chemistry of the office. I was trapped. I rationalized that Milt would have no problem finding employment, and Mike would go out and recruit someone just as good and maybe more palatable.

The next day Mike came into my office. He said that firing Milt was pure lunacy and asked me what I was going to do about it. I told him he should talk to Jane. He said he tried, but she stiffened and reminded him that she, not he, was in charge. I remembered that in my conversation with Jane, she mentioned that Mike had talked to her and she made it clear to Mike that the good-old-boys days were over and she was the boss. I think I detected a smirk on her face. Damn! Was I caught in a bind, and one of my own making! I explained to Mike what I thought. First, I was trying to empower Jane as a future executive and did not want to pull the rug out from under her at this stage of her career. Second, I said that Milt would have no problem finding work and Mike could find a replacement for him. Mike asked, "Is that it?" "Well yeah, is anything more needed?" "You're the boss." Mike shook my hand politely and seemed to be okay with my explanation. The next day I phoned Mike and asked him if he had started the search for a replacement and if he was in touch with Milt. He informed me that he had talked to Milt, who was pretty upset and that he, Mike, was looking around for a replacement and would keep me posted on the search.

Two days later it hit the fan. Jane called and tearfully told me that Mike had tendered his resignation. She had hoped that her conversation with Mike had cleared the air and she was looking forward to a good working relationship with him and everyone else in the office, now that Milt was gone. Now everyone in the office looked devastated, and they were angry at her. I assured her that I would personally address the problem with the rest of the office, and I would find a pathway out of jungle for her.

First, I called Mike to see if his situation was reparable. He informed me that he did not resign until he had secured a position at US Steel. It did not take long because the headhunters had been in contact with him and offered a better package than I had. He had stayed with us out of loyalty, but after Milt was fired, the loyalty was shattered beyond repair.

I said. "Sonofabitch Mike! You didn't give me any inkling that you might leave." He told me that Jane was acting like a hatchet woman and gave the impression that I would back her all the way. He told me he didn't dare say he might leave until he had another contract in hand. He also shared with me the unpleasant notion that people in the division suspected some hanky-panky between me and Jane. Mike said that because he knew me he didn't believe it, but when he tried to defend me the others just shrugged their shoulders or rolled their eyes like he was making a lame defense for an old homey. My own self-image as a leader had suddenly become wobbly, but I had to stay strong and move ahead.

My first move in damage control was to go to the engineering division and address them all as a group and then individually. I promised to listen to their grievances, to assure their job security, and in order to keep them on board, a salary bonus for those who stayed. As I said earlier, it was a very good department, and I wanted to preserve it. I thought the best way to preserve stability was to promote in-house. In my interviews with the department members, I asked them for input on an internal promotion. The consensus was for a guy name Jim Haught. He was affable and competent. He took the job that Mike had and we continued the search to replace Milt. Jane was "kicked upstairs" to a staff position, and we move ahead.

Jane was sobered rather than shattered by the experience. She was honest enough to know that her actions had been damaging although well-intended. She asked for my help in moving forward. I explained that my wife Kathleen had a lot of experience at helping young women launch successful careers and that she would be glad to help out. I also told Jane about the rumors of inappropriate activity between me and her, which we both knew were false. I arranged to have lunch in the company cafeteria very visibly with me, Jane, and Kathleen. In the end I utilized some contacts that I had at Alcoa and Jane got hired there. From what I have heard, she is doing quite well. She learned a lot and had a very expensive education—expensive to us.

In addition to problems of racial and sexual discrimination, the environmental issue was becoming prominent. As I studied the positions that were being tried or suggested there was one that I called "minimalist." The social responsibility of business meant compliance with federal, state, and local laws. David held this position. We could not turn Western Pennsylvania into somebody's notion of Eden, and we should not endanger profits and jobs by trying. I took a different position. Since we as an industry with our own engineers and scientists know more about the impact that we have on the environment than legislators do, we should look for cost-effective ways to exceed government standards and lead the way rather than just tag along. Further, if we can anticipate future regulations we will save money in the long run—what some writers like you call "Doing well by doing good." There was a lot of head-butting between David and me on this issue. Most of our executives and higher management favored his position. I never thought I should or could assume dictatorial powers, but I kept pushing back.

I informed the engineers as well as the production people that we would comply with all federal and state regulation, and further, search ways to cut emissions even more than the law required. I said this was not just do-goodism; it was also good business. If we stayed ahead of the industry and ahead of the law, we would not be blind-sided by future regulations that we weren't able to meet. We worked steadily to become more eco-friendly, but had some setbacks.

I learned of one of the setback when a turn foreman came to tell me of an incident that could get us in big trouble. A worker had given away a drum to a neighbor, who used it to burn trash. That was a problem in itself since the drum was not his to give away. But the worst part of it was that the drums had our name on them, and if one of the drums was misused to store or dispose of hazardous material, we would be blamed. The foreman wanted to suspend or fire the guy, but he was in his fifties and had a good record in more than thirty years of service. The foreman was looking to me for assurance that it was right to fire the guy. I told him not to fire the guy. Let him know that it was a fireable offense but that he would be given another chance. Also we could use this incident to teach everyone in the company that they needed to protect anything with our name on it. And they were not free to keep or give away any company property. I talked to the offending party. He was penitent and grateful to have another chance. He became somewhat of an environmental warrior for us.

In spite of our commitment to environmental responsibility, we had some serious problems. One of them occurred when a pump failed.

Two young technicians were monitoring a filter that removes hazardous waste from water that would be pumped back into the river. An emergency occurred when the pump failed and the toxic waste was rapidly filling up the compartment and threatening the expensive and necessary filtering equipment. The problem came on suddenly and quickly so that the technicians did not have the opportunity to consult with their turn foreman much less the environmental department. They had two choices: let the rising water ruin the equipment or release the untreated water in to river. They chose to release the water. As soon as they could they alerted the foreman who alerted our environmental and legal departments. This kind of problem was always kicked up to me, as it should be. We immediately alerted the state and federal EPAs who sent crews to clean up the spill. We were fined and made to pay for the clean-up, but because we acted promptly and honesty, environmental and legal damages were contained. The technicians were questioned and absolved of any wrong-doing. They were congratulated for their honesty and quick thinking. We upgraded the equipment to assure that such an incident would be the last of its kind.

Another incident, the mirror opposite of the one just described, occurred when an air monitoring device malfunctioned. The technicians entered numbers based on what they thought the device would have given. When the problem was fixed, they saw that the figures were reasonable and there was no problem. But there was a problem because an employee who was mad at the company and mad at the world, "blew the whistle." He informed the EPA that the figures were fake. We were fined minimally, and the agents understood what happened. The figures were reasonable and probably accurate. But the proper procedure, which the technicians were now schooled in, was to honestly report that the figures were unavailable until the equipment was back up and running. In spite of these relatively few problems, we had a good reputation for environmental responsibility and a well-earned relationship with the EPA.

Hard Times

In the early seventies, the competition from foreign steel companies became not only worrisome, but threatening. We had done well in terms of good pay and benefits for our workers, overcoming discrimination, environmental responsibility, worker safety, and quality steel. This was true of the entire American steel industry, and we at WPS were on the cutting edge. If we American steel makers were "the only game in town" as we were after World War II, our life would have been idyllic. Many of my confreres throughout the industry piously recited the capitalist creed that the economy is dynamic, that businesses works best when it involves risk, and that there are always winners and losers. But none of us really believed that this dynamic applied to us.

David and I had one of our regular debates about the whole purpose of industry. He claimed that we were in it to make a profit, to utilize capital in the most efficient way. Yes, he agreed, we have to obey the law and the normal requirements of ethics, meaning no force or fraud. But we cannot be sentimental or put vague ideas of social justice over our fiduciary duty to our shareholders. My response was that we were in business to make steel profitably, safely, justly, and in Western Pennsylvania. At this he made a gesture of banging his head against the wall, which he thought talking to me was sometime like.

The whole issues that the Board was looking at was that making steel in Pennsylvania was becoming prohibitively expensive. They argued that we should diversify our product and that we should look to moving the mill operation to where there are lower wages and fewer regulations. David warned me that the Board would look on me as a dinosaur trying to live in the 70s as if it were the 50s and 60s, "Times, they are a changing." That isn't what Bob Dylan meant by the phrase, but it applied here. I saw two conflicting ideas: We had to be profitable, and, at least in my mind, we had to continue making steel here, with this workforce, safely, and observing environmental safeguards. I had to think hard. How can I make this happen? How can I solve this conflict? Every conflict is resolvable. Right? In my happier moments I thought "We can do this." In darker moments I thought "I might strike out, but damn! I'll go down swinging."

I took time off to do some deep thinking. This was hard to do, like planning to drain the proverbial swamp when the alligators are already in your boat. But I had some good people under David's leadership to keep up the daily workings while I tried to see if there was some big idea that could save the whole operation. I remember conversations with Frank when he convinced me that good ethics is good business in the long run and that the application of wisdom to business is business ethics. Frank's reasoning was deeply rooted in his faith, and although I was not nearly as religious as he, I did have faith, and I believed that Frank's insights were not only correct but practical.

For most, or at least many, business leaders, ethics means nothing more than adherence to the law. Their codes of ethics as well as their ethical advisors emphasize compliance. I agree. But while compliance is necessary, it is hardly sufficient. Of course you have to do what you can to avoid fines, hostile court orders, and lawsuits. But that is not enough. You have to go beyond avoiding the negatives and actually nourish the positives. As I tell you this, I am probably channeling Frank. He had a great influence on my thinking and still does.

A lot of guys in business regress to childishness when they are talking about right and wrong. They might be mature persons in their private lives, I don't know. But in business, they act as if the name of the game is avoiding punishment. "Don't get the boss pissed off at you." Since I was the boss, they often wanted to make sure that they had my approval. But they wanted this approval from everyone ahead of them in the chain of command. Even when they were concerned about a wrong, that could be attributed to the company, they were concerned about punishment. If there was a dangerous situation, they wanted to remedy it, not because someone might get hurt, but because we might get sued or fined.

Some of them showed progress by identifying with the corporate culture. I was like this for many years myself. I liked our corporate culture and was instrumental in creating it. But much of my value creation was almost unconscious. I learned a lot from Kathleen as well as from Frank, Dave Craig and you, Jeff. We tried to treat everybody fairly and make a profit by creating a quality product, a safe work-place, and a responsible attitude toward the physical environment. I described this above.

Dave Craig thought deeper than I did at first. (Without bragging, I think my thought has since surpassed his.) But Dave made me aware of the universal aspect of law. We had to know and follow the law, not just to avoid fines and other punishment, but because the law provided a common set of values and guidelines. Laws are man made and not perfect. But they are laws. Dave and I had many conversations about whether it was ever right to break the law. We could not think on any example where civil disobedience would apply, and we could not think of many cases where breaking the law was justified. My conclusion was "When in doubt, obey the law." Dave looked at me as if to say "This is a close as I can get to making you understand ethics."

Dave held a deep devotion to the law. For him, following the rule of law did not just mean staying out of legal trouble. Of course it meant that, but much more. The law is an objective and universal plan that puts all of us on an equal footing. What we felt subjectively could not get beyond the fickleness of feeling. Our values held about as much consistency as the weather. But the law could serve as an unmovable moral compass. He reminded me that to make steel we had to understand the laws of chemistry and physics. And to run our business we had to respect "the iron laws of economics." But to do business ethically, we had to know and respect the letter and the spirit of civil law.

Although I knew that Dave was an elder in his Church and taught Sunday school, he did not, as they say, "wear his religion on his sleeve." But I think he saw the plan of God in history. His Presbyterian idea of predestination was not about God assigning people to hell, but about a vast plan in which we all take part. The duty of every person, not just Christians, consists in knowing as best we can, what God's plan for us will be, and fulfilling the plan to the very best of our abilities. The plan might not be what we want, or even what we think is best. But our duty consists in subordinating our subjective will to the universal and objective truth.

Specifically Dave was trying to make me see that my plan to keep making steel in Western Pennsylvania might not just be impractical, but even wrong-minded. When I told Dave that I thought he was being fatalistic, he informed me that those who believe in "fates" believe in blind forces which have no concern for the welfare of the human race. Dave believed in a benevolent providence. But he insisted that we have to bend our wills to the universal plan as we discern it, and not expect the universal laws to bend to our little wants and needs.

I understood Dave's reasoning and found it appealing. But I thought, and still think, that it was an abstraction that did not have the same value as the well-being of the workers, the community, and the relationships that owed their very existence to the operation of the mill. These relationship would be shattered if the mill were to close, and there would be an enormous amount of suffering, economically, psychologically, and spiritually. Sometimes I felt like I was Atlas trying to carry this whole world by myself. In the end I was unable to hold up. The world collapsed.

Dave was right. The Board brought in a committee of suits who were given the responsibilities that had been mine. I was reassigned and given an office in a building outside of Pittsburgh with some busy work to keep me out of trouble. I advised Dave to resign and take a job at Alcoa, which he did. The new masters of the operation began closing down and laying off workers. This happened quickly and brutally. I was now out of the loop and could do nothing about it.

The men, both labor and management, who had worked at the mill for their entire careers, thirty years and longer, had expected to retire at 65 with a nice pension. They would live in the community, in the very houses where they had raised their children who would take their place at the mill. In retirement guys hoped to hunt, fish, and tell stories of their time at the mill. Now this world was shattered. I kept thinking I should do something. Then I would realize that I had no power or authority and there was nothing I could do. Often at night I would dream that I had a solution, then wake up not even remembering what my dream-solution was. When I did remember, I realized it had no bearing on reality.

The whole community was devastated. There were editorials and letters to the editor spreading blame all around, and I came across as one of the bad guys. An editorial in the "Pittsburgh Catholic" pointed out that since I am a Catholic, I should have had a better understanding of Catholic Social Teaching.

It got worse. Many of the leaders of the union began blaming the Church for the problem. They especially singled out the Presbyterians because several of our board members were of that faith. These idiots terrorized children at a Christmas party, and a few months later disrupted an Easter Sunday service. Some of them thought I was a Presbyterian, probably because they assume that no Catholic could be a CEO. Then a group of ministers and their wives came from Iowa to help out some local ministers who took an activist stand.

The folks from Iowa were photogenic and articulate. They got a lot of TV coverage and explained that at one time they naively thought that job losses just happened. But then they studied economics, and now understand how things really work. The closing of the mill constitutes a deliberate and unnecessary decision by greedy corporate leaders. Their solution was even simpler than their analysis of the problem. Just expose the greed of the owners, and the public would force them to reopen the mills. They disrupted some Council meetings in several cities around Western Pennsylvania including Pittsburgh. The cameras were always present. At one time they even disrupted a union meeting, blaming the union leaders for collusion. If the TV cameras had not been there, I think the union guys would have kicked their butts.

There were a lot of man-in-the street interviews in which the reporter asked passers-by if they thought this "pro-labor" group had gone too far. Most people thought they did. If they had asked me, I would have said that the problem was not that they had gone too far, but that they were moving in the wrong direction. Nothing that they were doing could help keep old industry in the area nor bring new industry in. They seemed to think that just by getting TV time they were achieving something significant.

One of them, whose last name was Kuhlman, had a brother who had some singing and acting success and went by the name "Billie Cool." This song and dance man decided to make a documentary calling attention to both the plight of the workers and their families as well as the heroic effort of the ministerial group. In one eye-catching scene, they were to carry a rusty steel beam down the middle of the street and deposit in inside the Presbyterian Church. That would surely bring back the steel workers' jobs. The minister of the targeted church urged his people to avoid violence and confrontation of any kind. The Catholic clerics were silent on this issue and in their Sunday homilies talked about such things as adultery and pre-marital sex. Or the problem of nudity in the movies.

Maybe I was just looking for a fight, but this whole thing made me angry. As they walked down the street, they actually looked comic, and the episode should have evoked humor rather than anger. As they walked down the street, there were two camera men preceding them. Of course the cameras would not be seen in the finished documentary.

But I was not in a mood to laugh. I stood in front of the guys with the beam, took a firm grip on it and wouldn't let them pass. I was the seventeen-year-old football player once again.

They pushed, and I pushed back and they lost their grip. The beam fell with a loud clang and you could hear gasps and cries from the bystanders. It hit one of the guys in the foot and he was obviously in a lot of pain. My anger turned to concern. He didn't suffer any fractures or permanent injury, but needed stitches. Worse from their point of view—I spoiled their movie.

I was arrested for disorderly conduct. The police chief, my old classmate Lennie Sadasukas, made sure that I would not be photographed in handcuffs or being placed in the police car. He explained to me that he agreed with my position, but that these clowns had a parade permit. They would not have done anything illegal until they entered the property of the church, at which time they would have been arrested. I remember his words: "Damit Andy—leave these things to us—you spoiled our fun." I was fined and had to pay some damages, but the ministers declined the temptation to sue me. I guess that was the Christian in them.

The ministerial group disappeared from the public eye and the jobs did not come back. A lot of the children of the workers moved out of town to find jobs or took lower-paying jobs in retail. My dream of retiring from a thriving industry as an elder statesman was over. I look back upon my career with some disappointment but no regrets. I can't think of anything I might have done differently that would have saved the jobs. It took me some time, but I am fine now.

Charley McGinnis

My original plan was to have four narrations as depicted above. But after the project started, Charley said he would like to be included, and insisted that his perspective was needed to "prevent the reader from becoming diabetic by all the sweetness." I always referred to Charley as "dark Irish," not because of his complexion, but because of his outlook on life. So here is Charley's take on all of these things.

I KNOW YOU THINK OF me as "Dark Irish." I'm just realistic. I studied the history of Ireland and the migration to America, and I lack the historical amnesia and the fantasy images of our past. I never bought into the green plastic decorations and the sentimental songs about smiling Irish eyes. The first wave of Irish immigrants who came to this hemisphere were literally starving. They were loaded on to ships to serve as ballast; many died at sea and many others died from mal-nutrition and associated disease shortly after arriving. The ones who survived were greeted with hostility and violence which they returned in kind. Soon they got jobs as laborers, firemen, and cops. Many of their children went on to college staffed by religious orders who provided a solid but inexpensive education. So much for my postage-stamp ethnography

I should point out the obvious fact that a lot of Irish, especially in the big cities, became politicians. They provided good government, helped the poor, and were usually corrupt. Even in Frick we had our share, especially Big Jim Whelan. Now Big Jim was never accused of any kind of wrong-doing, but c'mon, he was an Irish politician. I really shouldn't say that, because Big Jim helped our family a lot and often pulled my old man's butt out of the fire. He did so literally when my dad was a rookie volunteer fireman with more guts than brains and Big Jim was the fire Captain. He also saved him from several metaphorical fires.

My dad was not as bad a guy as a lot of people thought he was. But when he was drinking, he became dangerous as all of us kids learned. I don't want to put the blame on him, but I became pretty aggressive myself—maybe it was in the genes. I fought with everybody. I remember sending you home with a bloody nose more than once. I even took on bad-ass guys like Andy Kuchar and Lennie Sadauskas. I got my butt kicked pretty good, but I never backed down.

I spent most of my teen-age years fighting and getting into trouble for underage drinking. During football season I behaved better to keep on the right side of coach Donatelli. I loved football because of the physical contact. After high school I enlisted in the Army. I thought, probably stupidly, that I would have liked going into combat, but had to content myself with being a Cold Warrior. I was good at driving trucks and operating heavy equipment and generally loved army life. I still drank heavily and got into a lot of fights. That was not a problem until I beat the crap out of my commanding officer. That merited me a less than honorable discharge.

I had married a girl whom I met in the Army. In civilian life I took a course in heavy equipment operation, and continue to do the work I love. Remembering the trouble that my dad's drinking caused our family, I quit drinking and have never been abusive to my wife or kids. So things worked out better than anyone would have predicted for me.

END GAME: Andy Builds a Beloved Community

AS I WAS EDITING MY notes and trying to put them into decent prose, I kept thinking about how to conclude the collection. I had several ideas, but then things suddenly changed. Andy called me and said he wanted to talk with me about something he thought was an important idea. He wouldn't go into detail on the phone, but I was interested. Knowing Andy, I was sure he was *not* going to do an Amway presentation.

When we met, he confided that he was undergoing a change in life that he was very happy about. Financially, he was well off. He had savings, a retirement package, and was doing a fair amount of consulting. But he said the core of his business career was over, and that he was now turning to a spiritual side. He said this side of his character was always there, but he thought he could express it through business leadership. This scared me a little, but his proposal was detailed, and I thought, realistic.

He wanted to start a group of like-minded people who would explore religion, philosophy, and spiritualty. We would all remain active in our overlapping communities and involved in working for social justice. He hadn't talked about his plan to anyone except Kathleen. She was as excited about it as he was and she knows a lot about how the human psyche works. Andy contacted me because I was writing the stories of our group and I could be what he called "The Rocking Writer" for this group. He then told me about other people he would contact. We talked about each of them and I drew up profiles of the role each would play.

He saw my Ruthie as a central part of this group. The observations about Ruthie were mostly Andy's. I am too close to her to have seen them, but after he pointed them out, I agreed. She is a kind of earth

"

goddess. Andy was not against pagan images, but thought that our group should have a Christian orientation. He suggested that she had Madonna-like qualities, not like plastic statues of Mary, but more of an active nurturing, maternal presence. Ruthie never liked adulation but usually responds to compliments with a simple "Thank you." She didn't want me to write this, but she tolerates me and always unselfconsciously puts her work ahead of her image.

Frank would be the best person to work out the philosophy and theology. He had the background and competence to do so, and he was rooted in reality so as not to drift off into meaningless abstractions. As Frank would be the intellect of the group, Joanne would be the heart. She had lived a lot, seen a lot of suffering, and endured a tragedy herself. But she is still the warm, hopeful, outgoing person whom we all knew and loved. I might add, although it is irrelevant, that she is still beautiful.

Next he would reach out to Dennis and Cecelia Keegan. Andy didn't want us to be a dull discussion group, although we would do a lot of discussing. But he wanted a dimension of music, celebration, and what he tried to explain with air quotes "theater." No one was more qualified to provide this dimension than Dennis and Cecelia. Besides, they were good people and old friends. The eight of us would be the core of the group without any formal title or office.

Besides, the core, he hoped to open it to all of our families, and as many friends who were interested. He wanted to include some non-Catholics like David and Phyllis Craig, and would talk to the Rabbi to see if he or any of his congregants were interested. Andy's brother Pete had stayed in the priesthood in spite of things seeming to fall apart around him. Andy thought he might be our chaplain and say Mass for us occasionally, although he would not put any pressure on him. Fr. Pete had enough pressure on him from every side.

So this was the beginning, the hopeful cast of characters, and now let me tell you how it unfolded. Most of our families expressed interest if not enthusiasm. Ruthie's brother Albert said he would help us in any way he could, but did not want to join us. He prefers a quiet, devout, Catholicism. Lennie Sadaskaus declined firmly. He said he still goes to church, "Every Christmas whether I feel like it or not." But I'm getting ahead of my story. We did not try to spread the word around until we established exactly what we wanted to do.

Kathleen, Ruthie, and I thought Andy was on to something and we were happy to be on the ground floor. The four of us met with Frank and Joanne to explain what we were trying to do and how Frank would be the main architect. He liked the idea and said he would try to come up with some basic principles, and then with the agreement and participation of all of us, we would flesh them out. He and Joanne also agreed that Dennis and Cecelia should be part of it.

So Frank got down to work. The eight of us would be a group, and as we brought other people in, we would help them organize into groups of about seven to ten people. We wouldn't be uptight about the numbers so that nobody would be left out. If groups of more than fifteen developed, we would encourage, but not require that they divide into two groups. Each group would be a faith-sharing group and would talk in confidence about their personal experience as well as discuss the readings for the following Sunday liturgy.

The whole community would meet monthly, or maybe bi-monthly, to learn more about an assigned book by a contemporary, theologian, philosopher, or spiritual writer. Four times a year we would discuss local problems involving justice so that we could look for solutions with local authorities. The members would belong to more than one parish, and hopefully include Protestants and Jews. We would keep in touch with the pastors or religious leaders and offer to be of assistance in their ministries. We, as Catholics, would develop our tradition and also encourage those of other traditions, to develop theirs. We would all learn from each other. We would emphasize the principles that unite us rather than those issues that might divide us. Frank quoted the

American philosopher, Josiah Royce, that our purpose in life is to move toward the "Universal Beloved Community."

Cecelia and Dennis agreed to lead the music and maybe some liturgical dancing. She played the piano, he played the guitar. They had three kids who played different instruments trumpet, saxophone, and clarinet. Others who played instruments would be invited to join them. Cecelia and Dennis could sing, they knew a lot of songs, and they were good song leaders. Music would take its rightful place. We would encourage members with other skills, such as painting or wood-carving, to integrate them into our meetings. We didn't say this out loud, but I think all of us, certainly me, were imaging this as the beginning of another Renaissance for the whole Church

A renewal was especially necessary for us because the pastor of St. Brendan belonged to a generation of young clerics who regretted the changes made by Vatican II. He insinuated as much Latin back into the Mass as the law would allow. (He probably thought the Greek "Kyrie" was Latin). In his homilies he never mentioned the environment, racism, or social justice. But he frequently talked about abortion as the great evil and urged his parishioners to vote for "Pro-Life" candidates. He always prefaced his political remarks by saying "Without getting political..." He often talked about faith by which he meant believing all the doctrines. "If you reject even one doctrine, you are not really a Catholic." It's not that people were rejecting doctrines, but that most did not even know what many of the doctrines were, and the doctrines did not impact anybody's spiritual or ethical life. For him, the central virtue of Christian life was obedience, and this included all the parishioners obeying him.

As we began meeting everything seemed to be going according to plan. The liturgies and other group meetings were lively and there was a warm family feeling among all of us. Joanne casually referred to it as "our beautiful community." There was wholeness, vibrancy, and even love among us. Our plans were flowing in a way that made us all happy.

Too happy, the cynic within me said, although I didn't say it out loud. But I couldn't help but think that life is not like this. It can be good, but not this good.

Charlie and his Daughter

We were wondering whether to invite Charlie McGinnis. We did not like excluding anybody, but Charlie had a knack for being disruptive. He solved the problem for us by coming up to me and letting me know he heard about our plans and thought it was one of the dumbest ideas he ever heard. Charlie asked if we were all going to let out hair grow long, put on sandals and tie-dyed t-shirts. How about a gaudily painted Volkswagen minibus? He described us holding hands, speaking of Jesus, and singing Kumbaya, and he laughed heartily at the image he described. One of the things I always liked about Charlie is that he had a great appreciation for his own wit and wisdom.

Charlie had four kids, a boy and three girls. The boy, Charlie Junior, was not a tough guy like his dad. He was more interested in music, poetry, and theology. While Charlie Senior had become a very traditionalist Catholic, his son moved away from the Church and claims to be "spiritual but not religious," a familiar phrase. For all of Charlie's disdain for what he called "pop-culture Irishness," he name his girls Tara, Erin, and Kerry.

His middle daughter Erin, came to me and could not praise our idea enough. She let me know how happy she was that we were doing this, how much she wanted to be part of it, how much she admired me and her dad's other friends, and how sure she was that her dad would eventually join. She was as Catholic as she could be. She knew which saint was honored every day, she made endless novenas, said all the mysteries of the rosary each day. And when she received Communion, she knelt down and received it on her tongue. But she was not narrow-minded. She liked all expressions of Catholicism, old and new, conservative and liberal. To her, the Church stood as a huge mansion in which there is room for everybody. As she phrased it, "Not many people know this, but the word 'catholic' means 'universal.'"

Erin made a triumphant entry into our group. She gushed about the love, joy, peace, and presence of Jesus that she experienced. But she thought she should do more. She remembered the passage in the Gospel about how some demons could be overcome only by prayer and fasting. So she would go on complete fasts. Kathleen was concerned that she might be anorexic. But Erin would go back to normal eating and never showed any sign of mal-nutrition. (We learned later that Erin was following a book on nutrition that recommended occasional fasting as a means of cleansing). She became very critical of the members whom she thought were not doing enough about poverty and racism. She would insult members, but then apologize saying that her approach was uncharitable. In her mind she was never in the wrong. She often reminded the group that more gifted people like herself had a duty to upgrade those who were not so gifted. She said she was aware that the truth hurts, but that nevertheless she needed to find more charitable way to tell the truth.

Erin became increasingly disruptive. We had been worried about her dad, Charlie, but the torch had been passed to a new generation. None of us wanted to crush her sprit, and we tried tactfully to get her to calm down. She mistook our tact for weakness and derided us for being such a bunch of marshmallows. Finally Andy told her that she needed to listen and learn and stop acting like "Little Miss Know-It-All," That did not go down well. I got a call from her dad accusing us of being a cult and brainwashing his daughter. He didn't stop with a phone call to me. He stormed into the pastor's office, we learned, telling him what evil was happening under his nose. The pastor was receptive because he thought by forming a group we were not showing him the proper respect. Charlie wrote to the bishop and even had a letter to the editor labeling all of our supposed mis-deeds and heresies.

Andy received a phone call from the pastor and a letter from a Monsignor in the bishop's office telling him to disband. If we did not, he would go to court to make sure that we did not use the word "Catholic" in referring to ourselves. (We never had used that term because we wanted to be ecumenical). Further, Andy was informed that excommunication had not been taken off the table. At an earlier time Andy would have been furious. But now, I think he was feeling more like Job. "The Lord giveth and the Lord taketh away." He did not want to do something divisive, so he recommend that we just disband as a formal group. We all remained friends. Even Charlie, when he saw any of us, was cordial as if nothing ever happened—he probably thought he had saved us from our own foibles. But the idea of a real Christian community was over.

How Will It End?

Several weeks after the community dissolved, Andy and Kathleen invited a group of us over. It was the eight who had been the core of the community. Besides Andy and Kathleen, it was Ruthie and me, Joanne and Frank, and Cecelia and Dennis. We had been friends since grade school and still felt a great affection for each other. It was a dazzling October afternoon on Andy's deck, with the sun setting behind a huge pin oak. We were sipping white wine and trying to see to what extent we could hold on to the golden days and how we could let go. I suggested that our theme song could be "The Class of 57 had a Dream." We all found this somewhere between appropriate and depressing. Ruthie had a better idea. She remembered a song that she, Joanne, Cecelia, and Kathleen used to sing a lot. "Such a Day as This Will Last Forever." They began to sing and after one verse we guys joined in. "Such a day as this will last forever, Such a day as this will always be." The moment summed up everything we had done, tried to do, or aspired to do. That day will last forever.

Did you love *Such a Day Will Last Forever: A Novella*? Then you should read *The Neglected Doctrine of the Holy Spirit: Josiah Royce as a Guide to Renewing Theology*[1] by Richard Mullin!

[2]

The Holy Spirit is a dimension of Godhood which is not given much attention, yet one that is critical for our spiritual development. In this work Richard Mullin shows how the contribution of American Philosophers at the turn of the 19th century can serve as a basis to reenvision theology. Importantly, he distinguishes the historical church with all its shortcomings and the Universal or "Beloved Community." Read this work if you are seeking a mature spiritual vision and one for which the church is a task that remains to be completed.

Read more at https://www.letphilosophyshine.com/.

---

1. https://books2read.com/u/3k51zO

2. https://books2read.com/u/3k51zO

Also by Richard Mullin

Ethics and the Full-breasted Richness of Life
The Neglected Doctrine of the Holy Spirit: Josiah Royce as a Guide to
Renewing Theology
Such a Day Will Last Forever: A Novella

Watch for more at https://www.letphilosophyshine.com/.

About the Author

Richard P. Mullin grew up in Carnegie, Pennsylvania, an industrial town in the Pittsburgh area. His father worked in structural steel, and his uncles and neighbors were nearly all blue-collar workers in local mills or the Pennsylvania Railroad. Richard earned his PhD in philosophy from Duquesne University, and taught philosophy for seven years at St. Bernard, a Benedictine college in Alabama, and for thirty years at Wheeling Jesuit University. He also taught Business Ethics in the MBA program at Wheeling Jesuit. Later he received an MA in Counseling from West Virginia University and worked in that profession as a contract counselor. He has three grown sons married with families, and he lives with his wife, Marian, in Wheeling, West Virginia.

Read more at https://www.letphilosophyshine.com/.